**Keely hesitated. "All my instincts
are saying that something isn't right."**

"Any sign of a dad?"

Keely shook her head, wishing Zack's gaze
wasn't quite so blue or so direct. It made it hard
to concentrate. "No dad. Mother mentioned a
boyfriend. The same person that the toddler said
pushed her."

Zach frowned. "I don't think you can rely on the
evidence of a two-and-a-half-year-old, Keely."

Keely took a deep breath. "I know that, but will
you just look at her?"

"I'll look at her." For a moment, their eyes
held and tension sparked between them, then
he muttered something under his breath and
strode off down the corridor, leaving her feeling
weak-kneed.

Dear Reader,

Perhaps you are driving home one evening, when you spot a rotating flashing light or hear a siren. Instantly, your pulse quickens—it's human nature. You can't help responding to these signals that there is an emergency somewhere close by.

HEARTBEAT, romances being published in North America for the first time, brings you the fast-paced kinds of stories that trigger responses to life-and-death situations. The heroes and heroines, whose lives you will share in this exciting series of books, devote themselves to helping others, to saving lives, to *caring*. And while they are devotedly doing what they do best, they manage to fall in love!

Since these books are largely set in the U.K., Australia and New Zealand, and mainly written by authors who reside in those countries, the medical terms originally used may be unfamiliar to North American readers. Because we wanted to ensure that you enjoyed these stories as thoroughly as possible, we've taken a few special measures. Within the stories themselves, we have substituted American terms for British ones we felt would be very unfamiliar to you. And we've also included in these books a short glossary of terms that we've left in the stories, so as not to disturb their authenticity, but that you might wonder about.

So prepare to feel your heart beat a little faster! You're about to experience love when life is on the line!

Yours sincerely,

Marsha Zinberg,
Executive Editor, Harlequin Books

ON THE MEND

Sarah Morgan

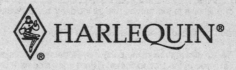

HARLEQUIN®

TORONTO • NEW YORK • LONDON
AMSTERDAM • PARIS • SYDNEY • HAMBURG
STOCKHOLM • ATHENS • TOKYO • MILAN • MADRID
PRAGUE • WARSAW • BUDAPEST • AUCKLAND

ISBN 0-373-51260-0

ON THE MEND

First North American Publication 2003

Copyright © 2001 by Sarah Morgan

This edition published by arrangement with Harlequin Books S.A.

® and TM are trademarks of the publisher. Trademarks indicated with ® are registered in the United States Patent and Trademark Office, the Canadian Trade Marks Office and in other countries.

Visit us at www.eHarlequin.com

Printed in U.S.A.

Sarah Morgan trained as a nurse and has since worked in a variety of health-related jobs. Married to a gorgeous businessman who still makes her knees knock, she spends most of her time trying to keep up with their two little boys but manages to sneak off occasionally to indulge her passion for writing romance. Sarah loves outdoor life and is an enthusiastic skier and walker. Whatever she is doing, her head is always full of new characters and she is addicted to happy endings.

GLOSSARY

A and E—accident and emergency department

B and G—bloods and glucose

Consultant—an experienced specialist registrar who is the leader of a medical team; there can be a junior and senior consultant on a team

CVA—cerebrovascular accident

Duty registrar—the doctor on call

FBC—full blood count

Fixator—an external device, a kind of frame, for rigidly holding bones together while they heal

GA—general anesthetic

GCS—the Glasgow Coma Scale, used to determine a patient's level of consciousness

Houseman/house officer—British equivalent of a medical intern or clerk

MI—myocardial infarction

Obs—observations re: pulse, blood pressure, etc.

Registrar/specialist registrar—a doctor who is trained in a particular area of medicine

Resus—room or unit where a patient is taken for resuscitation after cardiac accident

Rostered—scheduled

RTA—road traffic accident

Senior House Officer (SHO)—British equivalent of a resident

Theatre—operating room

PROLOGUE

'SAY that name again?'

Zach Jordan paused with a coffee-mug halfway to his lips, his blue eyes suddenly watchful.

'Which name?' His colleague Sean Nicholson, the senior consultant in the accident and emergency department, glanced down at the list he'd been reading aloud. 'Um…Keely Thompson?'

Keely…

Zach put his coffee-mug back on the table, untouched.

'What's the matter? Do you know her?' Sean frowned and Zach's eyes narrowed as he did the calculation in his head. Could it be her? Had that much time passed? Could she really be one of the new senior house officers—one of his hospital's new residents?

'I think I might,' he said finally. 'You interviewed her—can you remember what she looked like?'

Sean nodded and tossed the file of papers he was holding onto the table. 'I certainly can. Small and delicate, short blonde hair…a bit urchin like—massive blue eyes, the biggest smile I've ever seen…' He broke off and gave an appreciative grin. 'In fact, I have to admit that she was absolutely gorgeous, but don't tell Ally I said that.'

Zach gave an absent smile, knowing that Sean

7

adored his pretty wife and their three children. 'Bouncy? Bubbly personality?'

'That's her.' Sean picked up his coffee and took a sip. 'She's the daughter of *the* Professor Thompson from St Mark's. I suppose we should count ourselves lucky she's here. With that sort of pedigree I don't expect she'll be hanging around the Lake District for long. She'll be aiming for a job in one of the hot seats of academic learning.'

Would she? Zach gave a slight frown. That didn't seem like the Keely he'd known as a child. She'd been gentle and caring and totally lacking in ambition. In fact, there had been times when he'd wondered how on earth the Prof had managed to produce a child like Keely—she was so very different from the rest of them. But if she was following in the family footsteps and carving a high-profile career for herself then she'd obviously changed.

He sat back in his chair, wondering what she'd be like now. Last time he'd seen her she'd been a typical teenager, worrying about school and arguing with her mother. It was pretty hard to accept that she'd become a fully qualified doctor.

Sean was looking at him curiously. 'So how do you know her?'

'I trained with her older brother and sister.' Zach leaned forward and retrieved his coffee. 'They're twins. And one of my first surgical jobs was with the Prof. I used to go and stay with them sometimes. They had this fabulous house in the Cotswolds. That was where I met Keely.'

'She was the youngest?'

'Yes.' Zach gave a slow nod. 'The baby of the family. I wonder what she's doing up here in the Lake District?' If she was so ambitious, why hadn't she stayed in London? 'Can I look at her CV?'

He held out a hand and Sean passed it over. 'It's pretty impressive. Top grades all the way through.'

Zach studied it carefully. 'So did she say why she wanted to come here?' The hospital had a good reputation but it was hardly the most high profile in the country. Why hadn't she stayed in London?

Sean gave a shrug. 'I didn't really ask her that. Why shouldn't she come here? It's a great place. We love it. Why shouldn't other people?'

'It is a great place,' Zach agreed, frowning thoughtfully. 'But it's hardly the best springboard for a fast-track medical career.'

'You seem to know rather a lot about her.' Sean gave him a keen look. 'Did you have an affair with her?'

Zach choked on his coffee. 'For goodness' sake, Sean! She was sixteen years old and I was twenty-four! What sort of man do you think I am?'

Sean grinned. 'A woman's dream—if the gossip is to be believed. According to the nurses, you're now top of the list of the most eligible bachelors in Cumbria.'

'Oh, for Pete's sake, Sean!' Zach shot him an impatient look and put his mug down on the table with a thump. 'Since when did you start listening to women's gossip?'

'Since I lived with three of them,' Sean said ruefully. 'I'm decidedly outnumbered in my home and work life so I've decided to give in gracefully and adopt some of their habits.'

'Well, whatever gossip says, rest assured that I have more self-control and decency than to seduce sixteen-year-olds.' Zach was careful not to reveal the slight uneasiness Sean's words had prompted.

If it had been left to little Keely, they most certainly *would* have had an affair. She'd had a massive crush on him.

A ghost of a smile hovered around his firm mouth as he remembered the night she'd proposed to him. Turning her down without hurting her fragile ego had been one of the hardest experiences of his adult life.

What would she be like now? And would she have recovered from her teenage crush on him? If she hadn't then they were going to be in trouble.

Zach gave a short laugh, picked up the mug and finished his coffee. Of course she would have recovered. That was years ago, for goodness' sake, and he hadn't seen her since that night. He'd kept away— more for her sake than his. He'd decided that the sooner he removed himself from her life, the sooner she'd get over him and start fancying boys her own age. Which was probably what she'd been doing ever since.

'So come on, Mr Eligible Bachelor, bring me up to date.' Sean leaned back in his chair, a slow smile spreading across his face. 'Who's the lucky woman at the moment?'

'I thought you were one of the few people I could trust not to interfere with my love life,' Zach growled, irritation sizzling through his veins. This was one topic of conversation guaranteed to ruin his day. 'I have enough of it from your wife and the nurses in this department, without getting it from you, too.'

Sean looked at him calmly. 'Ally thinks it's time you got married.'

Zach closed his eyes and counted to ten. He loved Sean's wife dearly but he wished she'd stop trying to arrange his life. 'For the record, I am perfectly satisfied with my love life.'

'From what I've heard, you don't have a love life,' Sean said bluntly, 'just a sex life.'

'And since when was that any of your business?' Zach's blue eyes flashed a warning and Sean must have heard the threatening note in his voice because he gave a lopsided smile and lifted a hand.

'All right, all right. Calm down. I'm just saying that sooner or later you're going to have to take a risk and get back into a proper relationship.'

Sean was as direct as ever and Zach felt his hackles rise. Why did everyone feel they knew what was best for him?

'I have no intention of doing anything of the sort. I like my life as it is.'

There was a slight pause. 'It wasn't your life I was thinking of,' Sean said gruffly, not quite meeting his eyes. 'It was Phoebe's.'

Zach swore under his breath and stood up suddenly, the chair scraping on the floor as he pushed it away. 'Phoebe is fine.'

'Zach, she's not even three years old,' Sean said quietly. 'She needs a mother.'

Zach closed his eyes and the breath hissed through his teeth. Damn. Why did it still hurt so much? *Why?* It had been more than a year now. Were his battered emotions ever going to recover?

Sean gave a sigh and rubbed his forehead with long fingers. 'Look, tell me if I'm out of line, but—'

'You're out of line,' Zach said coldly, dropping his empty mug into the washing-up bowl. 'And, please, tell Ally I don't need her advice on my love life. And I certainly don't intend to get married again. There are some things you only do once in a lifetime.'

Sean studied his coffee. 'You say that now because you don't think you'll ever meet anyone again, but you will. Perhaps sooner than you think.'

Zach rolled his eyes. 'And I suppose this is the part where you tell me that you and Ally are having some people to dinner and I'm the available single man?'

Sean shook his head and grinned. 'I know when I'm beaten. I'm just going to let nature take its course. Once you meet Keely I'm sure you'll revise your opinion on romance.'

'Keely?' Zach blinked, thrown by the change of subject. 'What on earth has she got to do with this? Keely's a child, Sean.'

Why were they talking about Keely all of a sudden?

'A *child*?' Sean lifted an eyebrow and a ghost of a smile played around his mouth. 'She might have been a child when you last saw her but, believe me,

that was no child that I interviewed. Your ''child''
has grown into a woman. And a very beautiful
woman.'

Zach scowled. 'You shouldn't be making sexist
comments about the doctors who are coming to work
for you.'

'I wouldn't dream of making a sexist comment
when I'm working,' Sean defended himself
smoothly, 'but you and I are off duty at the moment
and as your friend I'm just telling you that your little
Keely is a knockout. Sweet, sexy and honest as the
day is long.'

'Then I'm sure she'll make some lucky man very
happy,' Zach said shortly, 'but it isn't going to be
me.'

Firstly, whatever Sean said to the contrary, he
couldn't think of Keely as anything other than a child
and, secondly, he knew he would never, ever find
another woman he wanted to marry. How could he
after Catherine?

CHAPTER ONE

WHAT had she done to deserve it?

Keely Thompson stared in disbelief at the man standing at the front of the lecture theatre.

She always helped old ladies across the road, she fed the birds in winter, she donated time and money to a charity for the homeless, she never told lies and she rang her mother regularly.

All in all she was a pretty responsible citizen and she definitely—*most definitely*—didn't deserve to bump into Zach Jordan again. Which proved that people didn't always get what they deserved, she thought gloomily, shrinking down in her seat and staring at her notepad. They got what they were given, and she'd been given Zach Jordan. Out of the blue, with no warning, and as her boss. Well, not exactly as her boss, but as a senior colleague, which was almost as bad.

When he'd walked through that door to deliver the lecture she'd felt as though she'd been hit by an express train. She'd been expecting one of the junior consultants from the accident and emergency department. She certainly hadn't expected Zach.

But it *was* Zach. And as it looked as though she was going to be a senior house officer in the same department as him, she had to come to terms with the fact that he was going to be under her nose. On a daily basis.

She stifled a groan and leaned her forehead on her hand so that he wouldn't be able to see her face.

So much for her escape plan. She'd chosen the Lake District because it was far away from home. And, most importantly, far away from people who knew her family. She'd needed space. Space and time. Time to think about what she really wanted to do with her life. She hadn't known that Zach would be here.

Zach, who knew her family almost as well as she did, and on top of that had been present, if not responsible, for the single most humiliating moment of her life. She'd been sixteen and he'd been twenty-four...

What was she going to say to him? How on earth did you greet someone you used to have a massive crush on and hadn't seen for eight years?

She moved her head slightly and peeped cautiously at the tall, broad-shouldered man standing at the front of the lecture theatre, totally at ease in front of his audience, his presentation style confident and relaxed.

Satisfied that he wasn't looking in her direction, Keely rested her chin in her palm and allowed herself the luxury of one long look at him. Over the years she'd decided that what she'd felt for Zachary Jordan had just been part of a teenage fantasy, but looking at him now all she could think was that she'd had impeccable taste when she was younger.

The man was lethally attractive. Smooth dark hair

swept back from his forehead, sexy blue eyes, a permanently darkened jaw and a body that made women drool. Zach Jordan was a real man in every sense of the word and at sixteen his looks had left her breathless. No other member of the opposite sex had affected her in the same way. She'd spent every minute of every day dreaming about how it would feel to be kissed by him.

He was the stuff of fantasies...

Obviously she wasn't the only one who thought so if the soft sigh from the female doctor sitting next to her was anything to go by.

'Wow! I thought doctors only looked like that in American movies. Tell me I'm not going to be working with him every day. I'll never be able to concentrate. I'm Fiona, by the way.'

Keely quickly introduced herself and picked up her pen. She wouldn't be able to concentrate either.

She shrank further into her seat as she remembered the way she'd behaved towards him as a teenager. The things she'd said to him. Like the night she'd proposed—

She suppressed a whimper of horror as she recalled that night. How *totally* humiliating. How on earth was she going to convince him that she wasn't a dippy teenager any more?

At least she *looked* different. Her blonde hair was shorter and somewhere along the road she'd grown a chest. And she was twenty-four now, for goodness' sake. Hardly the child who'd thrown herself at him all those years before. Maybe he would have forgotten all about it.

Staring at Zach was making her insides feel strange so she stared down at her lined pad instead and decided that the thing to do was to concentrate on making notes. It was certainly a better alternative than looking at Zach's broad shoulders—not that it was guaranteed to keep her mind on her work. There had been at least four occasions at school when she'd been given detention for scribbling 'Keely loves Zach' all over her notebook instead of paying attention.

Keely loves Zach...

Only she hadn't loved Zach, she told herself firmly, tapping her pen on the page as if to emphasise the point to herself. Not really. She'd just been a vulnerable, impressionable teenager and he'd been drop-dead gorgeous and very kind to her. A recipe for emotional disaster when you were sixteen.

She gave herself a mental shake and a sharp talking-to. She didn't have anything to worry about. She was a completely different person now. A grown woman and a fully qualified doctor about to take up her position as casualty officer in the accident and emergency department. She was long past the age of suffering from childish crushes. All she had to do was keep their relationship professional and prove to him that she was an excellent doctor.

With a determined expression on her delicate features she concentrated hard on that deep, sexy voice, making notes as he spoke about the medico-legal aspects of working in the A and E department, the importance of good note-taking and liaison with General Practitioners.

He was a good speaker, using just enough humour to keep their attention and just enough drama to make his talk interesting. Everyone was paying attention. Especially the women.

'He's unbelievable. I don't think I can work next to that man every day without throwing myself at him,' Fiona said dreamily, and Keely gave a wry smile. If her brother and sister were to be believed, women had been making fools of themselves over Zach since the minute he'd arrived at medical school, and probably long before that.

And hadn't she done exactly the same thing herself?

With a sigh her mouth softened into a smile and she remembered the first time her brother had brought Zach home to stay.

It had been love at first sight. On her part at least. Not on Zach's, of course. By all accounts he'd been used to cool, sophisticated women, and she'd been a smiley, chatty schoolgirl. He wouldn't have even *thought* of her in those terms. But still they'd been friends. And maybe they could be friends again—

She pulled herself together to find everyone in the lecture theatre staring at her expectantly.

'Dr Thompson?'

Oh, help! He'd asked her a question and she'd missed it. She'd been so intent on planning how to make him see her as a mature, qualified doctor that she hadn't been listening.

Her face heated and her palms were suddenly sweaty. So much for wanting him to take her seriously.

'I asked you to tell us where you worked last, Dr Thompson.' He repeated the question calmly and she swallowed.

'Medical,' she said breathlessly, glancing round with a self-conscious smile, relieved when he turned his attention to another of the new SHOs.

'I bet he's fantastic in bed,' Fiona said in an undertone. 'Look at those shoulders, those muscles, those legs—I feel faint just thinking about it.'

Keely felt faint, too, but for different reasons. This was never going to work. Zach was going to treat her the same way everyone else back in London had. As just another member of the Thompson clan, instead of as an individual. All the usual pressures would be there, the expectations—only with Zach it would be even worse because he was bound to remember her as a hare-brained teenager.

Was he going to think she wasn't up to the job?

With a long sigh she stared hard at her pad. Unlike her companion, she didn't want to look at Zach's body. She already knew how good it looked and the only way she was going to be able to work with Zach was if she *didn't* look at his body.

Suddenly she realised that everyone was standing up and shuffling papers. The lecture was over It was time to start work. And Zach Jordan was walking towards her...

She stood up and clutched her notepad to her chest, aware that her new colleagues were melting discreetly into the background.

'Hello, Keely.' The tone of his deep voice told her immediately that he knew exactly who she was and she felt hideously self-conscious. What on earth should she say? *Sorry I wasn't listening when you asked me a question. Sorry I proposed to you last time I saw you.*

'Hello, Dr Jordan—I mean Mr Jordan.' She'd suddenly remembered that he was a surgeon and corrected herself hastily.

A smile touched his mouth. 'Just Zach will do fine,' he murmured. 'We're very informal in A and E.'

'Right—well, what a surprise to see you.' She stroked a strand of blonde hair behind her ear and smiled brightly, wondering what it was about those blue eyes that made her revert to a stammering teenager. 'I had no idea that you'd be working here.'

'And is that a problem?' He gave a quizzical smile which made her knees feel weak and her heart misbehave.

'Problem?' Her voice squeaked slightly and she cleared her throat. 'No—of course it's not a problem. Why would it be a problem?'

She could think of a hundred reasons, starting with the physical effect he had on her. Just being in the same room as him brought her close to physiological meltdown.

'So what are you doing here?' He tilted his head speculatively. 'You're a long way from home, Keely Thompson.'

That had been the general idea when she'd chosen the Lake District.

'After six years in London I needed a change,' she said quickly, 'and I love mountains.'

She flushed under his steady regard, remembering that he'd always been perceptive. Could he read her mind? Did he know the real reason she was here? Had he guessed that she'd needed some space to make her own decisions, away from the influence of her family?

'Right.' He continued to watch her thoughtfully. 'And how are Prof and the twins?'

The inevitable question.

'Oh, you know,' Keely pinned a smile on her face, her response automatic. 'Fine. They're fine. Doing very well as usual.'

'I lost touch with Stephen,' Zach confessed, his blue eyes disconcertingly sharp as he looked at her. 'Doubtless he's made it to the top?'

Of course. Where else was there for her family?

'Professor of Immunology,' Keely muttered, still managing to maintain the smile. Just.

'And Eleanor?'

'Consultant Oncologist in London.' The smile was slipping but he didn't seem to notice.

'And the Prof? Is he retired?'

'Dad?' Keely's cheek muscles were aching and she gave up smiling. 'Oh, come on, Zach! Dad will never retire. His whole life revolves round being a professor.'

'I suppose it does.' Zach's voice was suddenly soft. 'And what about you, Keely? What's your chosen career path?'

Did she tell him the truth? That she didn't know? That the whole question of her future was driving her mad—

No, of course she couldn't tell him that! Zach was exactly like the other members of her family—clever, ambitious and totally driven. A born leader who had probably never known a moment of self doubt in his life. He was hardly likely to understand or sympathise with her plight, would he? She could hardly confess that she wasn't entirely sure what she wanted to do with her career—could hardly confide that she wasn't totally enchanted at the prospect of a career as a hospital doctor.

'Well, I'm doing six months of A and E before I commit myself,' she said finally, trying to sound suitably enthusiastic, 'but I'm thinking of doing cardiology. It's always fascinated me and we haven't got a cardiologist in the family.'

'I see.' He spoke quietly, his expression thoughtful, and for a moment she wondered whether he'd guessed that she wasn't being entirely honest.

'And do you think you'll enjoy A and E?'

She swallowed. Did he think she wasn't up to it? He'd already said he hadn't got used to the fact that she'd grown up.

'I know I'll love it,' she said firmly.

'Right.' Those blue eyes fixed on hers a moment longer. 'Well, if you have any problems—any worries at all—I want you to come to me.'

Oh, bother, he definitely didn't think she was up to it.

'I'll be just fine,' she said, a determined expression on her face. 'I'm really looking forward to A and E. It's going to be brilliant. I know I'll love it.'

He seemed amused by her enthusiastic outburst. 'It's nice to see you haven't changed.'

Well! Talk about tactless! Keely gaped at him. Did the man have problems with his eyesight?

'Of course I've changed!' She hoped that none of her new colleagues were listening to this conversation. How embarrassing! Being told she hadn't changed since she was sixteen was hardly flattering. 'Last time you saw me I had a flat chest, long hair and spots.'

He threw his head back and laughed. 'Actually, I wasn't talking about your physical appearance, I was talking about your personality. You always were smiley and good-natured.' His grin faded. 'I just hope you don't find A and E too stressful.'

'Zach, stop treating me like a child!' Keely was still put out by the fact that he didn't think she'd changed. She liked to think of herself as a cool cat. He made her sound more like a fluffy kitten. 'Of course I won't find it too stressful. I'm a doctor now! I'm not some child that needs to be nurtured.'

'I know that.' His voice was a slow drawl and he smiled again, obviously amused by her defensiveness. 'It's just going to take me a bit of time to get used to the idea.'

Oh, great. Then this was going to be every bit as bad as she'd feared when she'd first seen him stride into the lecture theatre.

She clutched her notepad harder and changed the subject. 'So, how long have you been working here?'

'In this department? Two years. I've been a consultant for a year.'

He was young for the post but, then, that was no surprise. He was every bit as bright as her siblings. In fact, she remembered Stephen sulking because Zach had beaten him in several exams.

'Well…' She broke off and cleared her throat. 'I don't suppose we'll see that much of each other, will we? I mean, there are four consultants in the department.'

'True.' His eyes gleamed. 'But we each work with three SHOs and you're on my team. We'll see plenty of each other, Keely.'

Her heart tumbled in her chest. How was she going to work with him every day without making a fool of herself? Just five minutes in his company had been enough to show her that the man still had a powerful effect on her. And what did *he* think of *her*? He'd admitted that he needed time to get used to the idea she was grown up. Did he think of her as the schoolgirl who'd proposed to him all those years ago?

She chewed her lower lip and decided she had to get things into the open.

'Listen, Zach…' She coloured furiously and glanced around quickly to check that no one was listening. 'About what happened when I was sixteen…'

His face was impassive but she thought she detected a brief twinkle in his eyes.

'I don't remember anything happening when you were sixteen.'

He was turning a blind eye to the fact that she'd made a total fool of herself over him.

'You're very kind, but I *want* to apologise. I've

wanted to for a long time.' She pressed on, determined to have her say. She couldn't work with him otherwise.

'There's really nothing to apologise for,' he said quietly, and she flushed.

'How can you say that when I—when I—' She broke off, totally swamped with embarrassment, and his face was unbelievably gentle.

'Had a crush on me? There's nothing to apologise for, Keely. These things happen.'

'Are you sure?' She looked up at him anxiously. 'You're not cross? You don't think it's going to be a problem between us?'

One dark eyebrow lifted. 'Why should it be? Unless you're planning to develop another wild crush on me.'

She was beginning to think it was entirely possible but she managed a laugh that she hoped sounded convincing.

'Goodness, no! I think I'm a bit beyond childish crushes now, Zach.'

And even if she wasn't, there was no way he was going to find out about it this time!

His eyes locked with hers. 'Good. Well, in that case we're not going to have a problem, and we won't mention it again.' He held out his hand. 'Welcome to A and E, Dr Thompson.'

With that he turned on his heel and left the room, leaving her staring after him. If he'd been handsome at twenty-four—and he certainly had been—then at thirty-two he was devastating.

Not that she was going to think about him in those

terms, she told herself hastily. She had made a complete fool of herself over Zach all those years ago and once in a lifetime was more than enough for anyone. This time she was keeping a strict control over her hormones.

She was *not* going to fall in love with Zach Jordan again…

Zach walked out of the lecture theatre and made his way back to the A and E department, his thoughts full of Keely.

He still couldn't believe it was her.

Last time he'd seen her she'd been little more than a child—and a very engaging child at that. He'd never been able to understand how her family had managed to produce a child like Keely. She was so totally different from the rest of them. Eleanor and Stephen were both like their parents—academic, emotionally reserved and totally driven.

But Keely… Zach gave a slight smile as he thought of how she'd been—Keely was warm, affectionate and slightly hare-brained. Unfortunately those qualities hadn't been valued enough by her family and he remembered several occasions when Eleanor and Stephen had given their little sister a hard time.

He frowned as he pushed open his office door and put the slides from his lecture back in the cupboard. But somewhere along the line she'd obviously changed if her career plans were anything to go by. Funny really. He wouldn't have thought she was the sort to be happy in a high-powered hospital career. But he was obviously wrong.

He flicked on his computer, checked his messages and then glanced out of the window towards the mountains. This late in January they were always topped with snow and the views from the hospital were breathtaking. He loved it here, but would Keely?

Zach frowned slightly as he remembered her breathless enthusiasm for her new job, her transparent embarrassment at seeing him again and her sweet concern that he'd still see her as a child.

Was she right?

Was that how he saw her?

To be honest, he wasn't really sure. Certainly it was hard to imagine her as a doctor and, frankly, he was distinctly uncomfortable about exposing her to some of the horrors that they saw in A and E. But was that because he saw her as a child? He didn't think so. It was more to do with her personality. Keely had a vulnerability about her that brought out all his protective instincts.

He could see immediately why Sean had found her attractive. It wasn't just that she was pretty, although she was. Very pretty. But her appeal went much deeper than just her looks. She had the widest, most compelling smile he'd ever seen, an infectious laugh and a warmth that wrapped itself around you like a blanket from the moment you met her.

And privately he thought she was going to find A and E work emotionally draining. Keely felt things too deeply to be able to successfully shrug off some of the incidents that burst through their doors on a daily basis. Which meant that he needed to keep a close eye on her. A very close eye on her indeed.

By the end of the week Keely was at screaming pitch.

He was driving her mad. Whereas her colleagues were left to their own devices until they shouted for help, every time she turned round Zach was breathing down her neck. It was doing absolutely nothing for her confidence.

She could do the job—she *knew* she could. But not if her every move was being watched.

She was going to have to say something. The trouble was, when? Working in A and E was fast-paced to say the least. So far they'd had very little time for cosy chats. Maybe today she'd pluck up courage…

Before she could work out how to tackle the subject without sounding defensive, the paramedics brought in an emergency and she and Adam, one of the other new casualty officers, were called to the resuscitation room.

Seconds later Zach slammed open the swing doors of Resus and joined them at the trolley.

'OK, what have we got?'

'Twenty-five-year-old male, overdose—we don't know what he's taken. He was brought in unconscious.' Nicky Roberts, one of the A and E nurses, briefed him quickly as they all swung into action. 'One of his friends found him. Said he'd been depressed lately but didn't know if he'd been taking any drugs. The ambulance crew put in an airway.'

'OK.' Stethoscope looped round his neck, Zach

started to examine the man, his movements swift and methodical. 'No gag reflex. Someone bleep the anaesthetist and let's give him some oxygen.'

Keely tried not to be impressed by the speed and confidence with which he worked as he took charge of the situation.

'He's got dilated pupils, a divergent squint and increased muscle tone and reflexes.' His eyes flickered past Keely and rested on Adam. 'Does that give you any clues as to what he might have taken?'

Keely ground her teeth. *He was doing it again.* Ignoring her and asking Adam the questions. Why hadn't he asked her? Why wasn't he treating her the same way he was treating the others?

Did he think she didn't know the answer?

She gave Adam a moment to speak but when he hesitated, clearly unsure, she stepped forward, her small chin lifting slightly as she spoke.

'Could it be tricyclics?'

Zach's gaze swivelled to her and she saw the flicker of surprise in his blue eyes. 'It could be.' He looked at her for a long moment, obviously unsure whether to question her further.

Keely took the matter in her own hands. 'Obviously you'll want certain tests done,' she said crisply. 'In my opinion he needs a drug screen and a blood glucose, BMG, ABG and U and Es.' She listed the necessary investigations and then held her breath, waiting for his response. Would he give her a row for interrupting when he'd asked Adam the question?

There was a long silence and then a ghost of a smile played around his firm mouth.

'Then you'd better get a line in and send off those tests.' He shifted his sharp gaze to one of the student nurses. 'Pulse and BP?'

Keely felt a rush of relief and reached for an intravenous cannula.

'Pulse is 110 and his blood pressure is 70 over 50,' the student nurse said quickly, flushing slightly as that hard gaze shifted in her direction. 'Wh-what are tricyclics, Mr Jordan?'

Zach jerked his head towards Keely. 'Dr Thompson will tell you.'

Was he testing her? Keely taped the cannula in place. 'It's a type of antidepressant. Unfortunately it's quite serious in overdose.'

'He's tachycardic and hypotensive,' Zach muttered, his eyes moving back to Nicky. 'And his skin is dry and hot. Check his temperature, please. I'm sure Keely's right and it's tricyclics. What do you think?'

Nicky shrugged and picked up a thermometer. 'You're the doctor, Zach.'

'That's never stopped you giving an opinion before.' Zach's tone was dry as he returned his attention to the patient. 'OK, is that line in? Well done, Keely. Let's give him a plasma expander—500 mils gelatin. Do we have a name for him yet? Address?'

'The friend was giving his details to Reception. We'll check,' Nicky said quickly, despatching another nurse to talk to the receptionist.

Zach drew breath and wiped his forehead on his sleeve. 'Someone contact the GP, please—find out what he's taking, if anything.' He glanced up as the anaesthetist strode into the room. 'Hi, Doug.'

His colleague gave a brief smile of acknowledgement. 'What's the story?'

'Overdose,' Zach said briefly. 'Don't know what yet. We're working on it, but we're guessing tricyclics.'

The anaesthetist rolled his eyes and snapped open the laryngoscope. 'Bloody antidepressants.'

'Quite.' Zach's gaze returned to his patient. 'He's got no gag reflex. I want to wash him out. We need to intubate him with a cuffed tube.'

'By "we" I assume you mean me,' the anaesthetist said dryly, and Zach grinned.

'I do indeed. I'm not rummaging around in someone's vocal cords unless I have to.'

The anaesthetist frowned and reached for an endotracheal tube. 'Isn't it a bit late for gastric lavage? When did he take them?'

'His friends saw him two hours ago and he was fine,' Zach said calmly. 'I want to try it and I want to give him some charcoal.'

'You're the boss.' The anaesthetist shrugged and intubated the patient quickly, using a cuffed endotracheal tube designed to prevent liquid accidentally entering the lungs.

'Great.' Zach lifted his eyes to Nicky. 'Let's wash him out. Keep 20 mils of the aspirate for a drug screen. Then I want 50 grams of activated charcoal down the tube. And let's do an electrocardiogram.'

His steady stream of instructions left Keely's head reeling and she watched in awe as he and Nicky worked together, their smooth teamwork a result of years of experience. Nicky seemed to anticipate Zach's every move without being asked and he was so calm and relaxed that Keely's admiration quickly turned to gloom. Would *she* ever be as confident as that?

'He's in urinary retention,' Nicky said quietly, and Zach nodded.

'That's common after a tricyclic overdose. Try supra-pubic pressure. If that doesn't work then let's put in a catheter. How's that ECG?'

He leaned over her shoulder, frowning as he saw the trace. 'Well, that pretty much confirms Keely's diagnosis.'

As if to prove the point the student nurse came back in at that point. 'I've spoken to the GP. He *was* taking tricyclics. Amitriptyline.'

'Well done, Keely.'

Zach's quiet words of praise brought a faint colour to her cheeks and she suddenly felt deliciously warm inside. Maybe she would be as confident as him one day. He was the consultant after all.

Zach lifted the ECG trace and stared down at it. 'All right, Keely, you're the one who wants to be a cardiologist. Take a look at that and tell me what you see?'

He handed her the ECG trace and waited while she looked at it.

'Prolonged PR interval and QRS widening.'

'Right.' Zach took the trace back. 'Consistent with a tricyclic overdose. Let's give him 8.4 per cent sodium bicarbonate.'

Nicky turned away to do as he'd instructed and Zach turned back to Adam. 'He needs to be admitted to the cardiac care unit for monitoring. Can you bleep the medical registrar and I'll have a word with him?'

Half an hour later the man was stabilised and had been admitted by the medical team.

'Will he live?' The student nurse stared at Zach, her eyes wide and slightly stunned.

'Probably. And he'll probably do it again,' Zach said calmly, folding the ECG trace and putting it carefully in the notes.

'You were amazing, Mr Jordan. You knew exactly what to do. You saved his life.' She stared at him with a mixture of awe and reverence and Keely felt some empathy with the girl. Watching Zach in action was a humbling experience. Not only was he clearly a skilled doctor but his cool self-confidence had transmitted itself to the rest of the staff. There was no panic with Zach around.

The student nurse was still round eyed with admiration and Keely saw Zach frown slightly as he registered her longing gaze.

How would he react? Would he demolish the girl? No, that wasn't his style. Look how kind he'd been to *her* for a start.

But she sensed that his style had changed over the years. The easy charm was still there on the surface but underneath she sensed a cynicism, a hard edge that hadn't been part of the Zach that she'd known all those years ago. Was it just maturity? Or something else? Had something happened to change him?

'Saving lives is what we do in A and E.' His tone

was matter-of-fact and a touch impatient as he addressed the student nurse. 'It's the job. Any of the doctors here would have done the same.'

Keely could tell by the look on the young nurse's face that she didn't believe him, that she'd suddenly turned Zach into some sort of god with supernatural powers.

Nicky had obviously noticed, too, because she dealt with the situation quickly.

'You're needed in the dressing clinic, Bella,' the A and E nurse said hastily, ushering the young student out of the room before she could say anything else.

Zach made no reference to the incident, instead thanking them all for their help and issuing a few final instructions to Nicky before striding out of the room to talk to the patient's friends who were waiting in the relatives' room.

Keely exchanged looks with Nicky. 'Does he have that effect on everyone?'

Nicky nodded as she started to clear up the debris in the room.

'Everyone female. They soon get over it when they realise he isn't interested.'

Keely threw some rubbish in the bin and tried to sound casual. 'Isn't he?'

'Never.' Nicky glanced up and shook her head slowly as she looked at her. 'Oh, no. Not you, too.'

Keely stiffened. 'What do you mean?'

'I recognise that expression on your face. I've seen it too many times before not to. Don't fall for him,

Keely,' Nicky warned, lowering her voice as she spoke. 'It's a quick route to a broken heart.'

Keely licked dry lips. 'Do lots of women fall for him?'

'What do you think?' Nicky pulled a face and tilted her head to one side. 'Zach Jordan is so good-looking he can't walk down a street without women getting neck ache as they stare at him. He's clever—very clever—and on top of that he's got this air of calm confidence that women find irresistible. Pretty devastating combination of qualities. Of course lots of women fall for him.'

'Is he married?'

Now, why on earth had she asked that question?

Nicky's expression was suddenly remote and discouraging. 'I can't discuss Zach's private life—it wouldn't be right. But take it from me, he's not available.'

Keely frowned slightly, wondering why Nicky hadn't just answered her question.

'Forget him, Keely. He's a colleague and nothing more.' Nicky opened a laryngoscope to check the bulb. 'I know he's good-looking but, like I said, falling for Zach is a quick route to a broken heart.'

Unfortunately her warning was about eight years too late, Keely thought gloomily as she ripped off her gloves and tossed them in the bin. She'd fallen heavily for Zach when she'd first met him and she had a nasty feeling that nothing much had changed. He still had the power to turn her insides to jelly.

CHAPTER TWO

'FANCY a drink?' Nicky opened her locker and pulled out her coat and bag. 'There's a lovely pub just across the road. Log fire, nice staff, dishy barman...'

Keely grinned. 'In that case, definitely.'

It had been a long and stressful day so maybe a drink was just what she needed. A drink and the chance to stare at a dishy man who wasn't Zach. With any luck she'd fall madly in love with the barman.

'I'll just give Fiona and Adam a shout,' Nicky said, fastening her locker and putting on her coat. 'They're both off now, too.'

Keely took a deep breath. 'And Zach?'

Nicky shook her head. 'Not Zach. Zach never joins us and anyway...' she frowned at Keely '...I've already warned you.'

'I know.' Keely wrapped a wool scarf around her neck and smiled brightly 'Just being sociable, that's all. He *is* one of the team.'

'At work, yes,' Nicky agreed, walking across the staffroom and tugging open the door, 'but out of work—no. Zach keeps himself to himself.'

Did he? Why?

Keely followed her down the corridor, waited while she hassled the two SHOs into joining them and then walked out into the bitterly cold January night and across to the pub.

The pub was warm and cosy and a welcome alternative to her chilly flat.

'I need to find somewhere decent to live.' Keely sipped her orange juice and passed her crisps to Nicky. 'Because I was living and working in London until last week, I didn't have much time to hunt around so I took the first thing I saw. Believe me, it's less than exciting and, frankly, the landlord gives me the creeps.'

'My wife and I are renting a house in Ambleside until we decide where we're going to settle,' Adam told them, savouring his beer with obvious enjoyment. 'What about you, Fiona?'

'Oh, I've got an aunt who lives about ten minutes from the hospital, so I'm staying with her for now. She's great fun, actually.' Fiona ripped open another packet of crisps. 'Where do the rest of the staff live?'

Nicky settled back in her chair and stretched out her hands towards the log fire. 'Well, the senior consultant, Sean, lives about fifteen minutes' drive away in a converted barn with his wife and three utterly delectable children. Zoe, the staff nurse you probably met today, lives with her boyfriend in Ambleside and I live with my husband in a cottage about ten minutes away towards the Langdales.'

'Nice. I want to live somewhere more rural. At the moment I'm stuck in a tiny flat in the middle of town.' Keely pulled a face. 'What I really wanted was to live in a rural retreat. You know, views of the mountains, sheep at the bottom of my garden and an appalling trip to work every time it snows.'

Nicky laughed. 'In other words, somewhere totally impractical.'

'That's me.' Keely beamed at her. 'I came up here to escape from the city. If I wanted the city I'd still be living in London.'

'So why the Lakes?'

Keely shrugged and took a sip of her drink. 'Because this unit has a good reputation and because I love walking.'

And because it was sufficiently far away from her totally oppressive family to give her some much needed breathing space.

'I like walking.' Nicky munched at the crisps. 'So does Sean. He was in the army before he trained as a doctor so he's a real expert at climbing and things. And Zach loves the outdoors too.'

That explained the athletic body...

'Well, I'm going to go and see some rental properties as soon as I get a free moment,' Keely muttered, pushing thoughts of Zach's body away and glancing at her watch. 'I suppose I'd better be going. I've got some serious studying to do.'

Fiona lifted an eyebrow. 'Studying?'

'Yes, studying.' Keely gave a wry smile, deciding to confess. Even though they'd only worked together for a week, she already liked her new colleagues enormously. 'The last time I saw Zach I was sixteen years old and he obviously still sees me that way. I need to impress him.'

'Sixteen?' Nicky put her drink on the table with a

thump and stared at her in amazement. 'How did you come to meet Zach at the tender age of sixteen?'

'He trained with my brother,' Keely said, carefully missing out that he'd also worked for her father. The less people knew about her family the better. 'He used to come and stay sometimes.'

'Wow.' Fiona gave her a saucy wink. 'I bet he played havoc with your hormones at sixteen.'

Keely managed a weak laugh. He was playing havoc with her hormones at twenty-four, too.

'Anyway, I clearly have to work harder to impress him than everyone else.'

Nicky frowned. 'I don't think that's true. You impressed him yesterday—you told him that the man had taken tricyclics.'

'Yes—and I was the one who didn't know the answer,' Adam reminded them with a sheepish grin. 'If anyone needs to go home to study it's me.'

'No.' Keely stared into her now empty glass. 'Zach doesn't see you as a teenager.'

Nicky wiggled her toes in front of the fire. 'If I were you I'd just be yourself. From what I've seen today you're going to make a great casualty officer. You're good humoured, you don't panic in an emergency, you're friendly to everyone and you're nice with the patients. Zach will see that for himself soon enough.'

Would he?

Keely wasn't so sure. After the way he'd reacted this week it was fairly obvious to her that Zach thought he needed to keep an eye on her.

She'd give it a few more days and then she'd have to have a word with him.

'There's been a pile-up on the motorway. Six cars. They've asked for a medical team. Zach, I'd like you to go.' Sean Nicholson glanced at the other casualty officers. 'And Keely.'

Keely felt a rush of excitement which died immediately when she heard Zach contradict him sharply.

'Not Keely. I'll take Adam.'

Adam?

Keely opened her mouth to protest and then shut it again, glancing instead towards Sean. Surely he'd object?

But he didn't. He merely gave a brisk nod. 'Fine. Nicky and I will get things ready here. Nicky, which of your nursing staff do you want to send?'

'Liz,' Nicky said promptly, and immediately everyone swung into action.

Seething with fury, Keely helped prepare Resus for a large influx of casualties and she liaised with Ambulance Control and the wards.

By the time the patients had been admitted and dealt with her shift was almost over, but she was determined to have a word with Zach. She thought she knew why he hadn't sent her out with the medical team, but she wanted to hear it from his lips.

'May I talk to you?'

He looked slightly surprised but he gave a nod and they walked towards his office.

'Were there any fatalities?' It was small talk but

she didn't want to tackle her problem in the corridor with the whole department listening.

'Two. Trapped inside one of the vehicles. It was the usual story—everyone driving too close together, bunched up in the fog.'

He opened the door to his office and she followed him inside and closed the door firmly behind them.

His eyes drifted quizzically to her hands which were still holding the door handle. 'So what's the matter, Keely?'

She took a deep breath. 'You're the matter. Or rather, the way you treat me is the matter. Why are you doing it, Zach?'

He looked at her warily. 'Why am I doing what?'

She gave him an impatient look. 'You don't ask me any questions, you don't let me see any complicated patients, you hang over me like a nursemaid and now you just refused to let me go out as part of an emergency team even though Sean obviously thought I was capable of it.' She ticked the reasons off one by one on her fingers. 'I know you don't trust me but I think you should at least give me a chance.'

There was a long silence and then he turned and walked over to his window, staring out into the darkness towards the mountains. 'I do trust you.'

'No, you don't!' She walked over to him, determined to make him look at her. 'You never let me work the way you let the other doctors work.'

'That isn't because I don't trust you,' he muttered, raking long fingers through his already ruffled hair.

Keely frowned, baffled by his response. 'Why,

then? If you trust me then why aren't you just throwing me in the deep end along with everyone else? Why wouldn't you let me go out as part of the emergency team? It's obvious that you don't trust my clinical judgement—'

'That's not true.' He frowned sharply, as if the thought hadn't occurred to him. 'From what I've seen, your clinical judgement is spot on.'

'So why…?'

He turned to look at her, his blue eyes suddenly hard. 'Because sometimes these pile-ups are dangerous and the medical team ends up operating in lethal conditions. You could have been sitting in a squashed car giving pain relief to some poor chap who was going to be trapped for hours, you could have been dealing with someone who'd been thrown through the windscreen…'

She swallowed, taken aback by his grim expression and by the harsh tone of his voice. 'But you sent Adam.'

He closed his eyes briefly and gave a sigh. 'Yes. I sent Adam.'

'Because he's a man?' Keely frowned. 'Because you don't think I can handle the stress? Why can Adam handle the stress better than me? I didn't think you were a chauvinist, Zach.'

He muttered something under his breath. 'I am not a chauvinist.'

'Then why did you choose not to send a woman into that situation?'

'I didn't choose not to send a woman.' His jaw was rigid with tension. 'I chose not to send *you*.'

'Me?' Keely stared at him. 'So you're saying you would have sent another woman, but not me.'

He held her gaze. 'Maybe.'

She felt bemused and frustrated. 'Because you think I'm a child?'

'No.' He shook his head impatiently. 'This is nothing to do with your age. More your personality.'

Keely's heart was thudding and her lips felt stiff. 'What's wrong with my personality?'

'Nothing's wrong with it!' He lifted a hand and rubbed his fingers along his forehead. 'You've got a lovely personality.'

'But?'

'But nothing,' he said quietly, sitting on the edge of his desk and watching her steadily. 'I just know how sensitive you are.'

Keely gave an outraged gasp. 'That is not fair! You don't know me at all—you're just remembering how I was as a teenager. I'm trying to learn and be part of a team, and you're stopping me. Anyway, why should it bother you if I *do* get upset? It's *my* problem, not yours.'

He held her gaze without flinching. 'It bothers me because I feel responsible for you.'

'Responsible for me?' She gaped at him. 'Why are you responsible for me?'

'Because you're miles away from your family—'

Her eyes widened. 'I'm a grown woman, Zach! Believe it or not, I don't need to keep running to Daddy!'

'Keely, I just don't want you hurt.'

She stared at him, touched and frustrated at the same time. 'But you weren't worried about Adam?'

'Of course not!' He gave a short laugh. 'Adam can take care of himself.'

'And so can I,' Keely said softly. '*So can I*, Zach. Whatever you may think of me, whatever your memory tells you, I'm completely grown up now. I don't need your protection, however well meaning.'

His expression was bleak. 'We see some hideous things in Casualty.'

'Then I'll see them, too,' Keely said firmly, pushing her blonde hair behind one ear. 'Please, Zach, this is ridiculous. All week you've been hanging over my shoulder, asking everyone questions except me, treating me like the teenager I used to be. I am not a teenager any more. This isn't even my first job. You're driving me mad.'

Zach winced and had the grace to look guilty. 'Have I been that bad?'

'Worse!' Keely scowled and then grinned, her natural good nature reasserting itself. 'But I'll forgive you if you stop policing my every movement.'

Zach walked towards her and stopped dead, his eyes scanning her face as if he was trying to see her for who she was and not for who he remembered her to be.

'I just don't want you hurt,' he said gruffly. 'I know Prof would want me to keep an eye on you.'

'He certainly would,' Keely agreed sweetly, 'but you never did what Prof wanted when you worked for him, so don't use that as an excuse. I distinctly remember him saying that you were the brightest, most frustrating doctor he'd ever worked with. You questioned everything and you took risks that made his hair stand on end. And those risks usually paid off.'

'OK. I take your point.' He spoke slowly, a wry smile playing around his firm mouth. 'You have a right to spread your wings, too. I'll stop treating you as a child. On one condition.'

'Which is?'

His voice was soft. 'If you have a tough day, you come and talk to me. As a friend. We all need someone to turn to in this department. I want to be sure that you won't bottle anything up just because you're trying to prove yourself.'

'I never bottle anything up—you of all people should know that.' She coloured slightly but decided that she might as well clear the air once and for all. 'If I was any good at hiding my emotions, Zach, I wouldn't have yelled at you just now and I wouldn't have proposed to you all those years ago.'

The corners of his mouth twitched and his blue eyes gleamed. 'I thought we weren't going to mention that again.'

She gave a groan. 'I know. You've been so discreet and I can hardly bear to think about it, it's so embarrassing. But I still feel that I haven't really apologised properly.'

'I've already told you you don't need to apologise.'

'Zach, *I proposed to you*!'

His blue eyes twinkled. 'It was a leap year, sweetheart. You were allowed to propose to me. I was very flattered.'

Sweetheart. The way he said it made her insides melt even though she knew it hadn't been meant in *that* way.

Keely pulled herself together and cleared her throat. 'Anyway, I apologise for behaving like such an idiot and embarrassing you.'

'You didn't embarrass me.' His gaze was steady on hers and for a moment she stared at him, her pulse picking up as she looked at the broad shoulders and the dark hair. He was seriously gorgeous…

She suppressed a whimper. Why did he have such a powerful effect on her. Why? She wasn't a teenager any more, but when she was with him she certainly felt like one.

No!

She wasn't making that mistake again.

She was *not* going to fall for Zach a second time.

'So that's agreed, then.' She made an effort to ignore the effect he had on her. 'You'll treat me like an adult and forget the fact that I once had pigtails and proposed to you.'

'It's a deal,' he said softly. 'Oh, and by the way— you look considerably better without the pigtails.'

For a moment their eyes held and she immediately forgot all her resolutions and allowed herself the luxury of one brief fantasy. *Zach looking deep into her eyes and telling her that he loved her…*

Oh, help! She was going mad.

'Right, then.' She backed away, forcing herself to break the spell. 'I'd better get back to work.'

As she closed his office door behind her she gave a low groan.

Working with the man was going to be a nightmare! She may have grown up but the reaction of her hormones was exactly the same as it had been when she was sixteen. The truth was that she couldn't be in the same room as Zachary Jordan without wanting him. Which meant that she had a very big problem.

She couldn't see a fracture.

Keely stared hard at the X-ray, half expecting something to suddenly appear, but it looked clear. Which didn't fit with what she'd discovered on examination. All her instincts told her that the wrist was broken.

So why was the X-ray clear?

Bother.

She was going to have to ask Zach's advice.

Which was a nuisance because she'd been successfully avoiding him all week. Although he was the senior doctor on her shift, she'd managed to deal with almost everything without his help.

She found him in Resus, talking to Nicky.

'Problems?' He lifted a dark eyebrow and she felt her heart stumble. Why did he have to be so good-looking? It was very distracting. If she was going to last six months in A and E she was going to have to develop survival strategies. Like looking over his shoulder when she talked to him rather than at his face.

'I need your advice.' She raked slim fingers

through her jagged blonde hair and gave him a brief smile. 'I've got this lady in cubicle one I'm not sure about. She fell on her wrist and all the signs are that she's fractured her scaphoid, but I can't see anything on the X-ray.'

'Scaphoid fractures are notoriously easy to miss on X-ray so you're right to ask for help,' he said quietly. 'What did you find on examination?'

'Swelling, pain on wrist movements, tenderness on direct pressure two centimetres distal to Lister's tubercle of the radius and on proximal pressure on the extended thumb or index finger.' Keely listed everything briskly and he nodded.

'What X-rays did you request?'

'AP, lateral and scaphoid views—was that wrong?' She felt a stab of anxiety. 'Did I miss something?'

'No, you did well.' There was a glimmer of surprise and admiration in his eyes. 'Better than most. Come on, I'll check the X-rays for you.'

Keely followed him down the corridor, struggling to keep up with his long stride.

He squinted at each of the X-rays in turn. 'Well, you're right. They're all negative. Let's examine her.'

He introduced himself to the patient, examined her thoroughly and then nodded at Keely.

'It's a scaphoid fracture. I agree with you. Well done for trusting your instincts.'

As usual his quiet words of praise made her feel as though she could have walked on water.

'But why are the X-rays clear?'

Whenever she was in doubt about a patient she took every opportunity to pick his brains and was rapidly finding out that Zach Jordan was a first-class teacher.

'The fracture isn't always visible,' he told her. 'Put her in a scaphoid plaster and refer her to the next fracture clinic. They'll X-ray again and it might be visible by then.'

She remembered her father saying that Zach Jordan was one of the most talented doctors he'd ever worked with and now she was seeing it at first hand. He was fast and confident, never doubting himself and always ready to do his best for each patient. She just wished she didn't find him so disturbing.

'He's married.'

Fiona, the doctor who'd sat next to her in the lecture theatre on that first morning, flopped into a chair in the staffroom, a gloomy expression on her face. 'Why are the good ones always married?'

'Who's married?' Keely stirred her coffee, her mind still on a nasty road traffic accident that had come in earlier.

'Zach Jordan.'

'Zach?' Her hand suddenly shook and hot coffee sloshed over the side of the mug. 'Oh, no!'

She stood up and fetched a cloth only to find Fiona watching her with a knowing expression.

'You, too...'

Keely walked back to the table. 'What do you mean—"you, too"?'

'You're obviously just as smitten as the rest of us.'

'Fiona, I just spilled my coffee,' Keely said calmly, carefully mopping up the mess she'd made. 'Why does that make me smitten?'

Fiona gave a wry smile. 'Because he has that effect on women. My entire body shakes when he comes into a room. Believe me, I can't hold anything hot within a hundred yards of the man.'

Keely laughed. 'Fiona, you're awful.'

'Well, all I can say is that she must be an amazing woman.'

Keely rinsed out the cloth and put it back by the sink. 'Who must be?'

'His wife.' Fiona curled her legs underneath her and settled herself more comfortably in the chair. 'Imagine marrying a man like that. Not only does he have the most luscious body I've ever seen but he's strong and cool-headed and a brilliant doctor. And so-o sexy. What a man!'

Keely frowned. Was Zach really married? And why should it bother her if he was?

A man like Zach was bound to be involved with someone. And it was really none of her business. It wasn't as if she had feelings for him. Not really. She was just struggling with the remnants of a powerful teenage crush.

'He called her sweetheart,' Fiona said dreamily. 'I heard him on the phone. And then he said he loved her. Can you imagine? Isn't that romantic? He didn't care who was listening, he loves her so much he just wanted to tell her. If you ask me, she's a very lucky woman.'

A lucky woman indeed. Whoever she was.

Keely had heard enough. She emptied the remains of her coffee down the sink, made a limp excuse to Fiona and left the room.

Why did hearing about Zach's love life bother her so much?

She frowned again. Her reaction didn't make sense. So she'd once had a crush on him. So what? That wasn't enough to make her feel as though she'd just had major surgery to her insides. Her emotions were just confused, that was all.

She walked back to the main area of Casualty and picked up a set of notes. Work, that was the answer. Bury herself in work and forget about Zach. He wasn't hers and he never had been. And she didn't want him to be, she told herself firmly. OK, so she found him attractive. But so would any woman with a pulse. It didn't *mean* anything.

'So, have you found somewhere to live yet?' Nicky flicked the switch on the kettle and turned to glance at Keely. 'You've been here three weeks and you're still living in that awful flat.'

'Awful?' Zach walked into the room in time to hear the last remark. 'What's awful about Keely's flat?'

'It's fine,' Keely lied, 'just not in the nicest position. I wanted to live in the middle of the country with a view of the mountains.'

'Your flat is not fine,' Nicky said firmly, ignoring the looks that Keely was giving her. 'There's damp on the living-room walls and your landlord is decidedly creepy. And he's bothering you, you know he is.'

Keely glared at Nicky but it was too late. Zach was suddenly still, his eyes watchful.

'In what way is he bothering you, Keely?' His soft tone didn't deceive anyone and there was a sudden silence in the common room.

'He isn't,' Keely said hastily. 'Not really. Nicky's exaggerating.'

'That's not true.' Nicky spoke up again and Keely closed her eyes.

She was going to kill Nicky when she got her alone!

'He keeps knocking on her door at all sorts of weird hours,' Nicky told them, oblivious to the furious glances that Keely was sending in her direction. 'I'm really worried about her. She needs to move out of that place.'

Zach's expression was grim. 'Keely? Is it true?'

Keely suppressed a groan. Oh, no. Now he'd get all protective again, and he'd just started to treat her like an adult.

'I think he's just a bit lonely,' she said lamely, and his mouth tightened.

'I'll get you a room in the medical block until you can find somewhere else.'

Without waiting for her reply he paced over to the phone and spoke to the accommodation officer. Judging from Zach's tone, they were less than helpful and when he finally replaced the receiver his expression was black.

'They haven't got anything at the moment—apparently they had a burst pipe last week and it's taking for ever to fix. We'll have to think of something else.'

'It's all right,' Keely said mildly. 'I've got two flats to look at on Friday when I'm not working. Thanks for trying but I'm taking care of it.'

He hesitated, his dark jaw tense. 'I'm not happy with you staying there—'

'It's fine, Zach,' Keely repeated firmly, conscious that Nicky and two of the other doctors were watching them curiously. And no wonder. Why was he making such a fuss?

'Well, if those flats don't come to anything, let me know. If you're stuck you can sleep in the doctors' room.'

They had a room where doctors could sleep if they were on duty at night, but it was rarely used.

'Thanks.'

Zach turned and walked out, and Nicky let out a long breath.

'Well, who's protective, then?'

Keely rolled her eyes. 'To Zach, I'm still sixteen and I probably always will be.'

With that she stood up and left them to speculate.

She was checking an X-ray later in the day when she heard Nicky shout from the corridor.

'Keely, I need a doctor—*now*!'

Keely was there in an instant, her heart pounding as she saw the toddler in the arms of a paramedic.

'She's fitting,' Nicky said quickly. 'It may be a febrile convulsion. Get her into Resus and I'll bleep Paediatrics.' A febrile convulsion was a fit brought on by a high temperature and was quite common in very young children.

'Are the parents here?' Keely took charge of the toddler's airway and gave her some oxygen.

'Not yet.' Nicky turned to one of the student nurses, her expression grim. 'Call Zach. Call Zach *now*!'

Keely glanced up in surprise. Why was Nicky in such a panic? It wasn't like her at all and everything was under control.

'It's OK,' she said calmly. 'I can handle this without Zach.'

'I know you can handle it,' came the reply. 'I don't need Zach for his medical skills.'

Keely didn't have time to question Nicky further.

'Let's give her some oxygen, please, and some diazepam rectally,' she ordered. 'Do we have any details? What's her name?'

There was a brief silence and then Nicky cleared her throat.

'Her name is Phoebe.'

Keely glanced up expectantly.

'Phoebe what?'

Nicky hesitated. 'Jordan,' she said finally. 'Phoebe Jordan. She's Zach's daughter.'

Zach had a daughter?

Oh, dear God.

Keely turned her attention back to the sick child, her heart thumping. 'OK, what's her temperature? Let's strip her off, give her some paracetamol and get a line in.'

Nicky looked doubtful. 'Should we wait for Zach?'

'No way.' Keely was adamant. 'We need to cool her down and find out what's causing her temperature. Can someone get a fan, please?'

Luckily Keely found a vein easily and secured a butterfly onto the tiny hand.

Only seconds later the doors to Resus slammed open and Zach strode into the room.

'What's the problem?'

His eyes fastened on the limp figure on the trolley and his face blanched.

'Phoebe?' He elbowed Nicky out of the way and bent over his daughter. 'Phoebe?' He glanced from one to the other. 'What the hell's happened?'

It was the first time that Keely had ever seen him near to losing his cool.

'It looks like a febrile convulsion, Zach,' she said quietly. 'We've checked her blood glucose and that's fine. Her temperature's 40.5. I've given her diazepam and paracetamol.'

Zach's expression was tortured. 'We need to get a line in—damn, I don't think I can do it to her.'

He gritted his teeth and Nicky put a hand on his arm.

'It's OK,' she told him. 'Keely's already done it with no problem. She was brilliant.'

'I need to take some blood for U and Es and FBCs and I think we should try and get an MSU.' Keely hesitated, knowing that she was increasing his anxiety. 'And maybe a lumbar puncture. We've bleeped

Paeds but we need to find out what's causing the temperature. Was she ill this morning?'

'I didn't see her this morning. I was working here last night.' Zach took a deep breath and then bent over the trolley, his powerful body in stark contrast to the tiny toddler. 'Daddy's here, sweetheart.'

The rough, protective tone of his voice made Keely's heart melt.

'Who was with her last night, Zach? We need to know if she's been unwell.'

Zach straightened, his expression grim. 'Her nanny. Speaking of which, where is she?'

Nicky licked her lips. 'It wasn't the nanny that brought her in…'

Zach went totally still, his voice lethally soft. 'So who brought her in?'

'An ambulance crew, and they were called by the staff of the nursery.'

'*Nursery?*' Zach's voice was like a pistol crack. 'What nursery?'

Even Nicky flinched under his biting tone. 'The nursery at the leisure centre. One of the staff came in with her. They're in Reception.'

'What the *hell* was she doing in a nursery?' Zach took a juddering breath, checked that his daughter was stable and then looked at Keely. 'Look after her.' With that he strode out of the room towards Reception.

'Ouch.' Nicky pulled a face. 'I think the nanny's in trouble.'

'Her temperature's coming down.' Keely checked the reading and nodded with relief, turning back to the little girl with a gentle expression on her face. 'Good girl. Hello, sweetheart.'

She stroked the blonde head gently and felt her heart twist. The child was gorgeous. Long, feathery lashes drifted against her smooth cheeks and her skin was baby perfect.

Right on cue the eyes opened—two blue replicas of Zach's—and Phoebe started to grizzle.

'Want Daddy.'

'I know you do. Daddy's coming in a minute.' Keely examined her quickly, looking in her ears and her throat. 'Hello—what have we here? One very red throat and a pair of very red ears.'

She put the auriscope back on the trolley. 'That's probably what's causing it.'

Nicky looked anxious. 'You don't think its meningitis, do you?'

Keely shook her head. 'I don't think so but they'll take a look at her in Paeds and do a lumbar puncture if they're in doubt. In my opinion she's got an ear and throat infection. Come and have a cuddle with your Aunty Keely.'

She swept the fractious toddler into her arms and cuddled her close, walking across Resus towards a little mobile that they had hanging from the ceiling.

'Here—look at this…' She was spinning the mobile when Zach strode back into the room, the strain showing on his handsome face.

'How is she?'

'Want Daddy.' Phoebe held out her arms and he took her instantly, holding her tightly against him, his eyes on Keely. 'Temperature?'

'It's come down a bit. Thirty-nine degrees,' she told him. 'We've given her some ibuprofen as well as the paracetamol.'

'Good.' He nodded. 'So what do you think?'

Keely was touched that he was asking her opinion on his daughter.

'Her ears and throat are red,' she said quickly. 'I think we should start her on some antibiotics, keep up the paracetamol, monitor her temperature and admit her overnight. But I suppose we need a paediatric opinion.'

'That's me.' A voice came from behind them and they both turned, Zach's face showing visible relief.

'Tony—thanks for coming yourself. It's my daughter…'

'No problem.' Tony put a hand on Zach's shoulder and it was obvious from the sympathetic expression on his face that the two men were friends. 'History?'

Zach breathed out heavily and rubbed the back of his neck. 'She was fine when I left yesterday lunchtime. I didn't go home last night—I was working—but I called the nanny this morning and she said that everything was fine. But it seems that she's been taking the child to a nursery when I've been at work so that she can use the gym—'

'Ouch.' Tony pulled a face and Zach's eyes were icy cold.

'Precisely. The nursery nurse who looked after Phoebe there said that she was fretful and hot this afternoon—they tried to call the nanny but apparently they couldn't get hold of her. Then the child fitted and they called the ambulance.'

'Right.' Tony nodded. 'So it seems as though we have a history consistent with a febrile convulsion.'

'That's what Keely thought.' Zach suddenly remembered Keely and turned to her with an apologetic frown. 'Sorry. You haven't met, have you? This is Tony Maxwell, one of the paediatric consultants.'

Keely gave him a smile, described her findings and then watched while Tony examined the little girl himself. Zach settled himself on a chair and held Phoebe while Tony looked in her throat and ears and listened to her chest.

'I agree with Keely. It's her ears and throat, Zach. I'd say admit her for observation overnight and we'll see how she is in the morning.'

Zach frowned. 'You want her to stay in?'

'Only because you'll be stressed out by the responsibility of having her at home,' Tony said quietly. 'It's hard to think rationally when it's your own—believe me, I know. I've got two and I'm a nervous wreck when either of them are ill.'

Phoebe whimpered slightly and Zach held her closer. 'Can I stay the night with her?'

Tony shrugged. 'Of course. We've got a spare side room at the moment. You can go in there with her. I'll go back now and tell them.'

Nicky followed him out of Resus and Keely was left alone with Zach.

Zach dropped a kiss on his daughter's blonde head and looked at Keely. 'Will you do me a favour?'

She swallowed. 'Of course...'

Anything...

'Once I've settled her on the ward, will you sit

with her until I've sorted out the nanny?' His expression was grim but Keely felt no sympathy for the woman. She deserved everything that was coming to her.

'Of course I will.' She felt suddenly awkward. Surely she wasn't the right person to be staying with his daughter. 'Do you want me to call your wife or something? I expect Phoebe will want to see her mother.'

Frankly she was amazed that the little girl hadn't already asked for her mother.

Zach stood up, his features stiff and cold. 'I don't have a wife, Keely. She died a year ago.'

CHAPTER THREE

THE only light in the room was a gentle glow from a lamp placed on the locker beside the cot.

Outside the wind howled and wrapped itself around the hospital, a sharp reminder of the cold winter weather which had suddenly descended on them.

Phoebe lay in the cot, dressed in just a nappy and covered in a cotton sheet, her breathing steady and even.

Keely sat next to her, head resting against the bars of the cot, waiting for Zach to return. At least the child was more peaceful now. Her temperature was down and she was sleeping deeply.

In the quiet of the room, with nothing but a sleeping child for company, Keely had plenty of time to think. And all she could think about was Zach and what he'd told her down in Resus.

His wife had died? Phoebe's mother had died?

Dear God, why? How?

Her heart twisted as she imagined just how hard it must be for Zach. Not only had he lost the woman he'd loved but his precious daughter had been left without a mother.

Instinctively she reached a hand over the side of the cot and stroked the soft blonde hair. The little girl felt cooler, thank goodness, and Keely reached out a hand and switched the fan off.

'How is she?'

Keely jumped as Zach's voice came from behind her, catching her by surprise.

'Oh—she's doing well, I think.' She fought the urge to fling her arms round him and hold him close. Crazy! As if a hug from a friend could even begin to make up for the loss of a loved one. 'She's cooler. More peaceful. Her breathing is better. Tony came a few minutes ago and checked her again. He doesn't think they need to do a lumbar puncture unless you disagree.'

Zach shook his head. 'No. I've just spoken to the nanny and she says that Phoebe was up in the night with a temperature.' He touched his daughter gently, feeling her skin, his eyes alert for any change. 'She's claiming that she didn't tell me this morning because she didn't want to worry me.'

'Well, that may be true,' Keely said softly, but Zach gave a cynical laugh.

'You think so? I'm afraid I don't have your faith in human nature. I think the reason she didn't tell me that Phoebe was ill was because she knew I'd be checking up on her during the day and that I'd find out she'd been putting her in a nursery.'

That had been puzzling her and she frowned slightly as she stared at him. 'I'm surprised the staff in the nursery were prepared to take her.'

'They had a letter.' Zach leaned his forearms on the cot and watched the little girl, his tone menacing. 'It was written on hospital notepaper and signed by me, giving full permission for Phoebe to be left with them.'

Keely gasped. 'She forged your signature?'

Zach nodded. 'That's right. Charming, isn't it?'

'What are you going to do?'

'I've already done it,' he said grimly, stroking a strand of blonde hair out of Phoebe's eyes. 'She's clearing her things out of my house as we speak.'

'Well, at least Phoebe looks as though she's going to be OK,' Keely said soothingly. 'That's the main thing.'

He was silent for a moment and then some of the anger seemed to drain away and a wry smile played around his mouth. 'You always manage to see the important things in life, don't you? That's what I always loved about you as a child. You were totally different from everyone else. While your family were clawing their way up the career ladder, you were skipping school to help out in the local children's home.'

Keely's eyes widened. 'How did you know about that?'

'Your horrified family told me.' He gave a short laugh. 'You were the first person in the family to see that there was more to life than studying, and it came as a big shock for them.'

She grinned. 'I was in big trouble.'

'I know.' His eyes glittered in the semi-darkness. 'You were for ever in trouble about something. But you always had your priorities right.'

'I don't know about that.' She blushed and stared down into the cot, a lump building in her throat. She didn't want to think about her priorities. She wasn't even sure what they were any more. 'She's beautiful, Zach. You're very lucky to have her.'

'I know that.' He gave a short laugh. 'But being a male single parent is no picnic I can assure you. Take now, for instance. I've got myself a sick child, no child care and a demanding job. I'm not quite sure how they're going to fit together.'

'It will work out,' Keely said softly, leaning her cheek against the cot. 'And, anyway, she's the thing that matters most—not your job. She's gorgeous.'

Zach smiled, the first real smile for hours. 'Actually, she's a total minx,' he said dryly. 'The only time she's quiet is when she's ill. I suppose it was only a matter of time until the nanny left, if I'm honest.' He gave a long sigh and shook his head. 'Phoebe can be pretty difficult. You know what children of this age are like.'

'I certainly do.' Keely looked up and returned his smile. 'Is there anyone who can help you with child care?'

He gave a shrug. 'Sean's wife Ally helps me out in an emergency but she works part time as a GP so she can't offer more than the occasional day or two. I suppose my housekeeper Barbara could do the days.' He frowned, obviously thinking it through in his head. 'She's a real grandmother figure and Phoebe adores her, but the problem is the nights when I'm working. I suppose I'll just have to advertise again, but the thought of trusting anyone with her horrifies me.'

Keely's brain was working overtime. 'I could do it,' she said impulsively, leaning forward in her chair and lowering her voice so that she didn't wake the sleeping child. 'You can put me on different night shifts to you so that one of us will be at home with her.'

'You?' Zach looked startled by the suggestion. 'Why would *you* want to do it?'

Because she could make his life easier. She couldn't make up for his terrible loss. Maybe no one would ever do that. But she could help him with the practical problems. All she had to do was convince him that it was a good idea.

'Why would I want to help? Loads of reasons.' Keely's eyes drifted back to the cot longingly. 'Firstly because I love children at this age and I know she and I would have fun together—'

His eyes were watchful. 'And secondly?'

'Secondly…' She paused and took a deep breath. It must be such a sensitive subject. Would he hate her mentioning it? 'Secondly, because I'm so, so sorry that you lost your wife.' She faltered slightly as she spoke, nervous that she might upset him. 'You must be feeling so awful. The last thing you need is to battle with practical problems. I can't bring your wife back, Zach, but I can try to make life easier for you and Phoebe. If you'll let me.'

She broke off and bit her lip, waiting anxiously for his response.

'You always were a sucker for a sob story, Keely Thompson.' He gave a long sigh and rubbed long fingers over his forehead. 'And what would we offer you in return?'

'Accommodation,' she said promptly. 'My land-lord is giving me grief. I need somewhere to live.'

It wasn't anything she couldn't handle but she hoped that it would be enough to make Zach accept her offer to help.

He was silent, indecision showing on his hand-some face. 'She isn't easy. She locked the nanny out of the house last week.'

Keely grinned, sensing weakness. 'How enterpris-ing. And how stupid of the nanny to put the front door between herself and a toddler.'

Zach still wasn't convinced. 'She climbs every-where—she's lethal—'

'Zach, I know what a child is capable of,' Keely said gently, and he breathed out heavily and shook his head slowly.

'I just think it's an imposition—'

'It's not an imposition. I'd love to do it if you'd trust me.'

'Trust you?' His brows locked together in a deep frown. 'Of course I trust you.'

'Well, that's settled, then,' Keely said in a cheerful whisper. 'After work tomorrow I'll pick up some things and move into the nanny's room. I don't know where you live so you'll have to draw me a map.'

'I live in the middle of nowhere,' he told her in a low voice. 'Are you scared of being on your own in the house?'

She shot him an exasperated look.

'Zach, you're doing it again! I *am* the babysitter,' she reminded him dryly. 'I'm not the one that *needs* the babysitter, remember?'

He raised his hands in the air and gave her an apologetic smile. 'Sorry. In that case, thanks for the offer. I accept gratefully, although I don't know why you're doing it so any time you start to regret it, please, say. I'll draw you a map and leave a key for you in A and E, and you can come over any time you like tomorrow. I've cleared it with Sean that I'm taking a few days off.'

'Good.' Keely nodded and stood up. 'And now I'll go and find you a cup of coffee and a sandwich. You look exhausted.'

'I am.' He sank into the chair she'd just vacated and stared at his daughter. 'Oh, and, Keely…'

She stopped on her way to the door and turned. 'What?'

'Thanks. For everything.'

For a long moment their eyes locked and suddenly she found it hard to breathe. Was it her imagination or was he looking at her differently—almost as if he was seeing her properly for the first time?

With a supreme effort she dragged her gaze away. She was imagining things. Deluding herself as usual. Only this time she had her emotions well in hand. Zach needed her help and Keely wanted to do everything she could to make his life easier. After all, that was what friends were for.

Zach's house was a gorgeous stone cottage nestling at the bottom of the mountains with nothing but sheep for neighbours.

Keely looked at the keys in her hand but decided to use the bell instead. Instantly there was a thunder of feet and then a crash and noisy crying. Keely winced. Obviously a poorly, fractious toddler. Zach had sent a message down to her earlier, telling her that they were discharging Phoebe and that he'd be at home, so it wasn't a surprise to find them there.

The door opened and she grinned at Zach. 'The cavalry has arrived.'

'Well, am I glad to hear that,' he muttered, his eyes showing how tired he was. 'She's lost her favourite bear and I can't find the damn thing anywhere.'

Keely frowned. The man hadn't been to bed for almost three days if her calculations were correct. Which just showed how tough Zach was—a lesser mortal would have collapsed by now and all he had to show for it was some fine lines around those gorgeous eyes.

'Go upstairs and run yourself a hot bath,' she suggested, plopping herself down on the hall floor next to Phoebe, who was still screaming and drumming her heels. 'And then go to bed. If I need help I'll yell.'

Zach hesitated. Keely knew that he wasn't going to leave his daughter without some evidence that she could cope with the situation, so she reached into her pocket and pulled out one of the toys she'd had the foresight to buy in the hospital shop.

She didn't say anything to the toddler, just started playing with the car herself, exaggerating the engine noises and giggling just to show what fun it was. Sure enough, the screaming ceased almost instantly and a tear-stained face lifted itself from the carpet to stare at her.

'Brrmmm…' Keely pushed the car towards the wall and was gratified when Phoebe knelt up and held out a hand.

'Phoebe's turn.'

'Great idea.' Keely passed her the car, and when the little girl started to play she glanced up at Zach. 'You see? We're fine. Now, go and have that bath. Then go to bed and get some sleep. If I need you, I'll call.'

He hesitated, obviously still unsure about leaving her in charge. 'She's a pretty difficult child to handle…'

Keely gave him a gentle smile. 'Sick toddlers are always difficult. Go to bed.'

'All right, if you're sure.' He paused, still reluctant to leave her. 'If you need me—'

'I'll call,' she finished quickly, rescuing the car which had become entangled in the hall curtain. 'Goodnight, Zach.'

She pushed the car back to Phoebe and Zach gave her a tired smile.

'I haven't got the energy to argue. She needs more paracetamol in two hours. Thanks, Keely.'

Keely watched him go and then got stuck into the task of occupying a very fractious toddler. Zach hadn't been joking, she thought wryly as she coaxed and cajoled the little girl into playing with her.

Two hours later she was exhausted and running out of ideas.

'Want Daddy,' Phoebe said flatly, plopping down

on the floor of the playroom which Keely had discovered at the back of the house.

'Oh, Phoebe, look, is this the bear you lost?' Looking round frantically for a distraction, she scooped up a large brown bear and handed it over with a flourish, relieved to see a smile light up the little girl's face. Thank goodness. Another crisis averted.

She quickly assembled a few other toys which she thought might be useful and then found the kitchen and made some tea for the child.

'No!!' Phoebe flung the toast onto the kitchen floor and Keely picked it up calmly and put it in the bin.

'Aren't you hungry? Don't you want anything at all?' She could see another tantrum brewing and searched quickly for another diversion. Fortunately, at that moment a cat jumped onto the window-sill and Keely silently blessed it.

'Look, Phoebe. Cat. What does the cat say?'

Phoebe looked doubtfully at the cat and her face started to crumple. 'Daddy. Want Daddy.'

'That isn't what the cat says!' Keely scooped her out of the high chair and gave her a hug. 'Cat says meow.'

Phoebe rubbed her eyes. 'Want Daddy.'

'I know you do, sausage,' Keely murmured, 'so here's what we'll do. We'll put you to bed, and later on Daddy will come in and see you.'

The poor mite was obviously still feeling poorly and upset by her trip to hospital.

Keely whisked her upstairs, bathed her and settled her in a fresh cotton T-shirt. She didn't want to put too much clothing on her in case she spiked a temperature again, and with that in mind she made herself a little bed on the sofa in Phoebe's room. Zach was too tired to listen out for the little girl tonight and at least she'd had *some* sleep the night before.

After two stories Phoebe snuggled into her bed, stuck her thumb in her mouth and promptly fell asleep.

Keely breathed a sigh of relief and tiptoed out of the room. Thank goodness for that! She cleared the debris from the bathroom and quietly pushed open Zach's bedroom door. Was he OK? Had he managed to get to sleep?

He was sprawled on his back on the bed, one arm across his forehead, his breathing even. Keely's heart twisted. The man hadn't even had the energy to get under the sheets. His dressing gown had fallen open, exposing a broad muscular chest covered in curling dark hairs.

He was going to catch cold.

Keely's mouth dried as she reached out a hand to pull his dressing gown over him. Her fingers lightly brushed his warm skin and she pulled away as if she'd been scorched. The urge to touch him was so powerful it shocked her, and she curled her fingers into fists, curbing the temptation. She wasn't going to fall for Zach again, she reminded herself firmly. She was here to help him, not to make a fool of herself all over again. That sort of behaviour was in the past.

Gingerly she lifted the edge of the duvet and tried to fold it over him, but it was trapped under his powerful body and wouldn't budge.

Maybe she could find a blanket in one of the other rooms.

Averting her eyes from his hard jaw, dark with stubble, she backed out of the room, searched the bedrooms and eventually found a spare duvet which she placed over him.

Then she checked Phoebe again, cleared the kitchen and went to bed herself. Ridiculously early, of course, but she was sure that the little girl would need her in the night so she wanted to sleep while she could.

She was in his child's room.

Zach stood in the doorway, his eyes resting on the slim figure of the woman asleep on the sofa.

When he'd woken up he'd gone straight to Phoebe's room to check on her and then searched the house for Keely. He hadn't even noticed her asleep on the sofa in his daughter's room. He just hadn't expected her to be there. Why would she do a thing like that?

Why hadn't she just made herself comfortable in the guest room and left him to listen out for his daughter? And why had she bothered to cover him with a duvet when he was asleep?

Because that was the sort of person she was. Warm and giving. A real nurturer.

Zach gave a sigh and allowed himself the luxury of looking at Keely. She was gorgeous. That blonde hair, cut in a jagged, modern style that suited her so well, and those long, slim legs curled up on the sofa cushions. And she was even smiling in her sleep. She looked very young and very vulnerable and she was right when she accused him of treating her as a child. He *was* treating her like a child. He had to. Because if he didn't treat her as a child, he'd treat her as a woman—and if he treated her as a woman...

Damn.

He shouldn't be thinking that way about Keely.

As he stood in the doorway she stirred and then gave a gasp of fright as she saw him.

'Oh, Zach, you made me jump!' Her soft whisper made him smile and he walked over and crouched down by the sofa.

'Keely, you don't have to sleep in here. That sofa will give you backache. Go and sleep in the guest room.'

She rubbed her eyes like a sleepy child and stifled a yawn. 'What time is it?'

'One o'clock, and thanks to you I've had eight hours' uninterrupted sleep so it's your turn to get some rest.'

She shook her head. 'I'm fine. Honestly. And so's Phoebe. She had paracetamol before she went to sleep, she drank some milk and seemed fine. She hasn't woken up once. I took her duvet off and gave her blankets instead because I didn't want her to overheat.'

She'd thought of everything.

Zach felt an unfamiliar sensation tug at his insides. He lifted a hand and stroked the tempting strands of honey blonde hair that fell in a tousled mass around her pretty face, telling himself firmly that what he felt towards her was just gratitude.

She froze under his touch and stared at him like a rabbit in a trap. 'Zach?'

Her hair felt incredible. Soft and sensual, a silky curtain of temptation that he wanted to touch for ever.

Still groggy from lack of sleep, she looked totally adorable, her huge blue eyes bemused and unfocused as she looked up at him.

Driven by an impulse outside his control and beyond his understanding, he bent his head, his mouth hovering only a breath away from hers while he made a final valiant attempt to resist temptation and listen to common sense.

He saw her eyes widen, saw the question in them and then he was kissing her. Really kissing her, the way a man was meant to kiss a woman.

And she *was* a woman.

He knew that now.

There was no way he could pretend otherwise.

There was nothing childlike in the way she was responding to his kiss.

Nothing childlike in her warm, womanly response which made his guts clench and his heart thunder in his chest. He was drugged by the taste of her, by the seductive touch of her lips, and he deepened the kiss, exploring every inch of her soft mouth.

Kissing Keely.

It was something he'd never even allowed himself to contemplate. She'd always been out of bounds. The baby sister of his classmates.

But she wasn't a baby any more…

Without breaking the kiss, Zach scooped her up in

his arms and sat down on the sofa, settling her on his lap so that he could have better access to her body. He felt her shiver with reaction and soothed her gently, one hand stroking her arm, the other locked in her hair, holding her head steady for his kiss.

He felt her hand reach up and part his dressing-gown and then rest tentatively on his hard chest.

Still blocking out common sense, he mirrored her action, slipping his long fingers inside her dressing-gown and touching the soft swell of her breasts. He was surprised by how full she was for such a slight woman, and her body's immediate response to his touch made the blood race through his veins.

'Drink!'

Pheobe's cry was like a cold shower and Keely gave a soft gasp and wriggled off his lap, leaving him to fight for control.

Damn.

What had he been playing at?

He ran a hand over his face and shook his head slightly to clear it.

'She's not hot. She was just thirsty.' Keely didn't look at him and Zach could tell by the dark stain on her cheeks that she didn't know what to say to him. Which was hardly surprising, because he didn't know what to say to her either.

What the hell had come over him?

'I'll sort her out. Go to bed, Keely.' His voice sounded rough. Rougher than he'd intended. 'I'll stay with her now. You need some sleep.'

Why had he done that?

Why had he kissed her when he'd known it was madness?

Because he'd lost control. And he couldn't remember the last time he'd lost control with a woman. He never lost control. Even when he had relationships—and he was becoming more and more choosy as time went on—he always managed to keep himself emotionally detached. In fact, since Catherine's death it was as if his heart had been replaced by a block of ice. He seemed incapable of feeling anything for anyone except Phoebe.

So why had he reacted so strongly to Keely?

Zach gritted his teeth and settled his daughter back in her bed. Maybe if they just ignored what had happened it would go away. They'd both been tired and worried about Phoebe, that was all. It hadn't meant anything. But he'd better make sure she understood that. The last thing he needed was Keely developing another crush on him. She wasn't the sort of woman to settle for a brief affair and he was in no shape to give anything more. He had nothing to offer a woman like Keely.

Keely walked hesitantly down the stairs the next morning and then froze when she heard laughter in the kitchen. She couldn't do it. She didn't know what to say. Turning quickly, she started to go back up the stairs, but it was too late.

'Keely?'

Zach had obviously heard her footsteps. Bother. No escape.

Now what?

What did you say to a man who'd kissed you senseless the night before and then behaved as if it hadn't happened?

'Hi, there.' She flashed him a bright smile that probably looked as false as it felt and walked briskly down the stairs as though passionate kisses in the middle of the night were an everyday occurrence. 'How's the invalid this morning?'

'Come and see for yourself.' He'd pulled on a pair of tracksuit bottoms and a loose-fitting sweatshirt, but he obviously hadn't bothered to shave. He looked breathtakingly handsome and Keely's heart thumped against her chest and threatened to obstruct her breathing.

Oh, help, it was happening all over again. She was falling for him.

No. No. No! She gritted her teeth and told herself firmly that she was doing no such thing. She was bound to find him attractive—what woman wouldn't? But that didn't mean she had real feelings for him.

She followed him into the kitchen and smiled at Phoebe who was sitting in a high chair at the table, demolishing the remains of a boiled egg.

'Hello, cherub.' Keely sat down next to the child and touched her forehead. 'You feel cool. More paracetamol?'

Zach shook his head. 'Not since the dose you gave last night. I think she's getting better.'

'Phoebe poorly,' the little girl said clearly. 'Poor Phoebe.'

Zach grinned. 'Poor Phoebe, indeed.' He ruffled

her hair and sliced her toast into fingers. 'At least you're more cheerful this morning.'

Phoebe wrapped her chubby fist around a piece of buttery toast and held out her arms to her father. 'Want cuggle.'

'Cuggle?' Keely frowned and then nodded. 'Oh, I see—she wants a cuddle.'

'Finish your breakfast first,' Zach said firmly, but Phoebe started to whine and grizzle and eventually he scooped the messy toddler onto his knee, ignoring the lumps of butter and egg that attached themselves to his clothing. 'There we are, then. One cuddle coming up.'

Keely swallowed hard and reached for a piece of toast. Just seeing the two of them together turned her insides to marshmallow.

'Awful parenting, I know,' Zach said with a rueful smile, finishing his own toast as he balanced Phoebe on his lap. 'I should have been stern and made her stay in her high chair until she'd finished eating. I over-compensate all the time, I'm afraid.'

'Don't apologise Zach. You're doing a great job,' Keely said quietly, spreading butter on her toast. 'A really great job.'

Zach watched her for a moment and then pushed a mug of tea towards her. 'Here—this is yours. You deserve it after last night.'

'Thanks.'

'It's me who should be thanking you,' he said quietly, and she concentrated on her toast to hide her blush.

What exactly was he thanking her for? Kissing him?

Probably not.

'You're welcome,' she said finally, glancing up and giving Phoebe a smile. Anything rather than look him in the eye. 'Presumably you're not going in today?'

'No.' He shook his head. 'I don't want to leave her with anyone until I know she's better, but I'm going to talk to Barbara, my housekeeper, about looking after Phoebe during the day. I might go in tomorrow if she's all right.'

Keely took a sip of tea. 'I'm off tomorrow, so I'll look after her then if you like. Just to make sure that she really is on the mend before you give her to anyone non-medical.'

Those blue eyes were suddenly wary. 'Keely, there's something I need to say to you...'

Oh, help. She could guess what was coming.

'You want to talk about the kiss,' she said lightly. 'But it's OK, Zach. We were both tired. It didn't mean anything.'

There was a brief silence. 'And you're all right about that?'

'Of course,' she lied bravely. 'Why wouldn't I be?'

He gave a sigh and tilted his head against the back of the chair. 'Because, to put it bluntly, you once had a crush on me and last night I did something I shouldn't have done. I don't want you to get the wrong idea.'

He was obviously afraid she was going to throw herself at him again.

Well, she wasn't.

She'd never make that mistake again. She couldn't stop herself from finding him irresistibly attractive, but she *could* stop herself from showing it.

'Look, it was just a simple kiss,' she pointed out gently, and he gave a short laugh.

'In my experience there's no such thing. I need to spell this out, Keely, and if I hurt you then I'm sorry.' He took a deep breath and his expression was serious. 'I am not in the market for a serious relationship.'

She nodded slowly, her eyes sympathetic. 'Because of your wife?'

His jaw tightened and he stood up quickly, the chair scraping on the kitchen floor. 'Because of Catherine, yes.'

'You don't have to talk about it, Zach.'

'No.' His voice was harsh. 'And, frankly, I don't want to. Suffice it to say that any relationships since her have been…superficial.'

Superficial?

Presumably he meant just sex.

Suddenly a lump grew in her throat. What was it like to love someone that much? So much that no one could ever take their place.

A muscle worked in his lean jaw. 'Don't fall for me, Keely.'

'Relax. I got over that when I was sixteen.'

He didn't look convinced. 'You're all right about living here? After last night?'

'Why shouldn't I be?' She gave a shrug and reached across the table to give Phoebe some more toast. 'I'm old enough to handle one kiss without falling into a swoon and expecting you to marry me.'

'You're making light of it but I just want to make sure you're clear—'

'I'm clear.' She held his gaze and smiled. 'I understand the main house rules. Residents must *not* fall in love with the master of the house. Any other rules I should know about?'

He visibly relaxed and shook his head. 'No. Aren't you going to be late for work?'

She looked at the kitchen clock. 'Oh, help. Probably! I'd forgotten I had further to drive this morning.' She stood up and waggled her fingers at Phoebe. 'I'll see you later.'

'If you have any problems today, talk to Sean,' Zach told her, frowning slightly as she picked up her bag and keys and flew towards the door.

'Yes, boss.' She grinned and opened the door, letting in a stream of icy cold air. 'See you later.'

She climbed into her little car, trying to ignore the leaden feeling in her stomach. It was all very well telling herself that she wasn't going to fall for Zach, but after that kiss... But it hadn't meant anything, she reminded herself firmly. It might have been breathtaking, and fantastic, and all the things that kisses were meant to be in fairy-tales, but it hadn't actually *meant* anything. There hadn't been any feelings behind it—at least not on Zach's part.

Zach was obviously convinced that he'd never love another woman again, and maybe he was right.

Maybe for him there would never be another woman who matched up to his first wife. Certainly he'd just gone to great pains to make sure that she hadn't misunderstood the situation.

And she hadn't.

She understood perfectly.

Falling for Zach would be a quick route to a broken heart, just as Nicky had told her, and she had no intention of putting herself through that twice in a lifetime.

CHAPTER FOUR

'YOU'RE KIDDING!' Nicky stopped dead, her arms full of sterile dressing packs. 'You've *moved in* with him?'

'Why are you so surprised?' Keely caught the dressing packs before her colleague dropped them on the floor.

'Well…because… He never…' Nicky gaped at her, almost speechless, 'Zach never, *ever* lets women stay at his house. In fact, to my knowledge, he's never introduced any woman to his daughter—apart from the nannies, of course.'

Which was exactly what Zach had told her himself.

'Yes, well, that's where I fit in,' Keely said lightly, tossing the packs into the box in the treatment room, ready for the dressing clinic. 'In Zach's eyes I'm somewhere between a child and a nanny.'

Or at least she had been before last night.

'Even so, I cannot believe he's letting you stay with him.' Nicky straightened her uniform and took a deep breath. 'Maybe there's hope after all.'

'Hope for what?'

'Hope for Zach. Hope that he might one day allow himself to get involved with a woman again.' Nicky frowned. 'Frankly, he's so emotionally detached that

I didn't think he'd ever let anyone get close to him again.'

'Don't get carried away, Nicky,' Keely said dryly. 'I'm staying in his house to help look after his child, not him. I'd hardly say we were close.'

It was true. Zach might have kissed her but she wasn't any closer to the real Zach than she'd been when she'd arrived. Nicky was right when she described him as emotionally detached. He certainly was. But, of course, now she knew the reason. Part of him was locked away after the death of his wife.

Nicky shrugged. 'I still think it's a step in the right direction.'

Keely lowered her voice. 'He—he told me about his wife.'

'Did he?' Nicky sighed. 'Awful, isn't it? I don't know any of the details—it all happened before he came to the Lakes.'

'He must have loved her very much.'

'Yes. He certainly isn't interested in another serious relationship,' Nicky agreed, opening a new box of sterile needles. 'But what about you, Keely? Are you sure you're going to be able to live with the man without falling for him?'

'Honestly?' Keely gave a rueful smile. 'No, I'm not sure. But if I do fall for him I promise not to let it show.'

Nicky shook her head. 'Don't let yourself be hurt, Keely.'

'It's Zach who's hurt,' Keely said simply. 'And if I can make things better by helping out in a practical way then I will. Don't worry about me. I can cope with my feelings.'

At least, she hoped she could.

Zach was bathing Phoebe when he heard Keely's cheerful greeting from the hall.

She was home.

He lifted Phoebe out of the bath and wrapped her in a towel, ruthlessly pushing aside memories of Keely's soft mouth under his. The way she'd felt…the way she'd tasted…

Damn.

He should never have kissed her.

He'd thought of nothing else all day and, despite his blunt warning to her this morning, he knew that the kiss was going to cause him no end of problems. She was going to expect something he couldn't ever give a woman again.

He walked into Phoebe's bedroom, slap into Keely who was obviously looking for them.

'Oops. Sorry.' She grinned and steadied herself against the door, leaning forward to kiss Phoebe. 'How is she?'

'Much better, thanks.' Zach moved past her, trying not to notice her flushed cheeks or her happy smile. If he looked at her smile then he'd see her lips, and if he saw her lips he'd want to kiss them again…

What on earth was the matter with him? He never normally had any trouble resisting women. In fact, he'd become something of an expert at keeping them at a distance. Why was Keely proving so much of a temptation? She wasn't even his usual type, if he was honest. Normally he ended up with cool, sophisticated women—like Catherine. But Keely was nothing like Catherine. Maybe that was it. Maybe he was attracted to Keely because she was as unlike his first wife as a woman could possibly have been.

'Why don't I put her to bed?' Keely reached out to take Phoebe from him, but she squirmed away and clung to her father.

'Sorry. Don't take it personally.' Suddenly Zach felt exhausted. 'She's always been quite clingy. She doesn't go to people very easily.'

'Well, that's understandable,' Keely said softly, a sympathetic smile on her face. 'Phoebe, shall we go and look out of your bedroom window? We might see that cat again.'

Phoebe stiffened and looked suspiciously at Keely. 'Cat in garden?'

'Maybe.' Keely nodded and gave the little girl a smile. 'What do you think? Shall we go and look?'

Phoebe hesitated and then nodded and reached out her arms.

Zach hid his surprise and watched as Keely settled his daughter on her hip, still chatting about the cat.

Damn, she was good with children. Incredibly patient and good-humoured. He knew only too well just how difficult Phoebe could be, but Keely didn't seem bothered by her behaviour. Just incredibly understanding. And smart. She always had a distraction ready, something to capture the little girl's interest.

'You could pour yourself a drink and put your feet up.' Her eyes were twinkling at him and he frowned and shook his head.

'You're the one that's been at work all day.'

'And work is nothing compared to looking after a toddler, as we both know,' she said with a laugh. 'Go on. We're going to look for the cat. Pour me a glass of wine while you're there and I'll be down in a minute. White, please.'

But he couldn't move. Seeing his daughter cuddled close to a woman made his insides twist.

'Are you OK?' Keely's voice was soft and her eyes were concerned. 'Zach? Have I done something?'

'No. You haven't done anything,' Zach said roughly, 'and I'm fine.'

Damn.

It wasn't her fault that his emotions were in a mess. But he was going to have to be more careful in the future. He knew what Keely was like—if she guessed just how raw he was inside then she'd be trying to mother him and sort him out. And that was the last thing he wanted.

'Daddy poorly,' Phoebe said emphatically, and Zach gave a wry smile and ruffled her soft blonde hair.

'Daddy's not poorly,' he reassured her gently, stiffening as Keely touched his arm, her expression still worried.

'Do you want to talk about it?'

'Nothing to talk about.' He detached himself from her touch and walked towards the door. 'I'll go and pour the drinks.'

It was typical of Keely to think that talking would solve his problems, typical of her trusting, optimistic approach to life. He most certainly didn't want to discuss his feelings with her and he had no intention of dumping his hurt or bitterness in her lap. He didn't want to use her in that way. She was still young and naïve enough to believe that relationships could end happily ever after. Who was he to disillusion her?

He gave a short laugh. And anyway, if he was honest, talking was the last thing on his mind. What he *really* wanted to do was drag her into his bedroom and have his wicked way with her. Lose himself in that gentle warmth and amazing passion which he'd glimpsed the previous night when he'd kissed her—

Which was out of the question, of course.

Keely wasn't that sort of person. For all he knew, she might even still be a virgin. But whether she was or wasn't, she certainly wasn't the type to go to bed with a man unless she was emotionally attached. And emotional attachment was definitely off the agenda.

Keely hesitated in the doorway of the kitchen, unsure whether Zach would welcome her presence. He'd been very short with her upstairs and she wasn't entirely sure why, although she could guess. Seeing another woman getting close to his daughter must be hard for him, even if she was only a friend.

So what should she say?

Deciding to keep it neutral, she stepped into the kitchen and settled herself at the table.

'Nice smell.' She gave an appreciative sniff and rested her chin on her palm as she watched him cook. 'What are we having?'

'Nothing exciting.' He reached into the fridge and

removed a bag of ready-prepared salad. 'Lasagne OK with you?'

'More than OK. I love it. Is this mine?' She leaned forward and picked up one of the glasses of wine that he'd poured. 'Zach, I don't expect you to cook for me if I'm living here. I can look after myself.'

He shrugged. 'It makes sense to eat together if we're both in.' He threw a smile over his shoulder. 'Don't worry, it's your turn tomorrow.'

'Deal.' She grinned and took a sip of wine. 'I love your house, by the way.'

'Do you?' He put the food on the table and settled himself opposite her. 'I like it, too, but some of the nannies have found it a bit isolated. It's hardly close to the local nightspots.'

She chuckled. 'Are there any?'

'A few.' He handed her a spoon. 'Help yourself.'

Keely helped herself to a generous portion of lasagne. 'So how many nannies have you had?'

'Four in total. It's been a nightmare.' He heaped salad onto his plate and pushed the bowl towards her. 'The first one stayed two months, the second one managed eight months, which was pretty good, the third one stayed one month—that was bad—and the last one, well, you know about her.'

His mouth tightened and Keely pushed his wine towards him.

'Don't think about her,' she advised. 'Why did the others leave?'

'Various reasons. Phoebe was difficult—missing her mother.' His tone was casual but a faint colour touched his hard cheekbones and Keely frowned at him suspiciously.

'And?'

'What?' He took a slug of wine and glanced up at her, his expression remote.

'There must have been more to it than that. A professional nanny should have been able to cope with one little girl, however difficult.' Keely's eyes widened as the penny suddenly dropped. 'It wasn't Phoebe, was it? It was you. They all fell in love with you, didn't they?'

He gave a short laugh. 'I wouldn't exactly put it like that.'

She put her fork down and stared at him. 'Oh, Zach, that must have been the last thing you needed.'

'That's an understatement.' He stabbed his salad with more force than was warranted. 'It certainly made it difficult for Phoebe. Every time she got used to a nanny, I had to get rid of her.'

Ouch. More reasons for him to avoid women.

'Did they cause you real trouble?'

'Yes.'

His economical response made her smile. 'Go on, give me the gory details.'

'You want details?' He sighed and sat back in his chair. 'All right. I found number one lying in my bed, waiting for me, when I came back from the hospital one night. That was tricky.'

Keely gasped and covered her mouth with her hand. 'Oh, Zach! What did you do?'

'Not what she wanted me to do,' he said dryly. 'Number two was slightly more subtle. She made my dinner every night and finally burst into tears and said that she couldn't carry on living with me unless I married her because she was so in love with me.'

'Ouch.' Keely pulled a sympathetic face. 'And number three?'

'Number three was virtually a repeat of number one but slightly more pornographic.'

'Oh, dear.' Keely put her fork down and started to laugh. 'Maybe you should have recruited an older nanny?'

'You think I didn't try that?' He drained his wine and stared into the empty glass. 'Unfortunately they all have their own families and don't want to live in. With the demands of my job, I need someone to live in.'

Keely picked up her fork and started eating again. 'Talking of which, did you manage to speak to your housekeeper today?'

'Barbara?' He nodded. 'Yes. Thankfully she's only too happy to help. She adores Phoebe and really wanted to look after her but couldn't offer before because she couldn't cover the nights.'

Keely's eyes twinkled. 'And will you be safe from your housekeeper or are you likely to find her lying naked in your bed?'

His smile was wry. 'She's fifty-six with two grand-children of her own, so I think that the only thing she's likely to be doing with my bed is making it.' He cleared his plate and pushed the dish towards her. 'Have some more.'

'Thanks, it's delicious.' She spooned more onto

her plate and noticed him watching her curiously. 'What?'

'It's just very refreshing, being with a woman who eats. Normally women pick at their food.'

'Don't remind me. My appetite is my biggest failing,' Keely told him gloomily as he topped up their wineglasses.

'Why? You hardly need to watch your weight—you've got a fabulous figure.'

Her eyes lifted to his and she blushed gently at the reminder that he was fairly intimately acquainted with her figure after the kiss they'd shared the previous night.

They stared at each other for a long moment, awareness sizzling between them. Then Zach stood up abruptly, his chair scraping the floor as he moved away from the table.

Keely took a deep breath and tried to slow her pulse rate. They'd gone from comfortable to awkward in the space of a second.

'Listen, Keely…' He turned to face her and his voice was rough. 'About last night—'

'We already discussed last night, Zach,' she reminded him calmly, 'and you made your position quite clear.'

A muscle worked in his jaw. 'I was wrong to kiss you—'

'Stop worrying,' she said quietly. 'It was just a kiss. This may come as a surprise to you but I have been kissed before. Please, don't think I'm reading anything into it. We were both worried about Phoebe and weird things happen to common sense in the middle of the night.'

He sighed and ran a hand through his hair. 'Maybe, but that's no excuse on my part. I should have shown some self-control.'

She was glad that he hadn't. Which was ridiculous, of course, because that kiss had left her wanting something she knew she couldn't have.

'I don't know why you're worrying. Let's just try and forget it,' she suggested lightly, standing up and loading her plate into the dishwasher.

'Can you do that?'

She looked him straight in the eye and summoned up her best acting skills. 'Of course. I've already told you that I've moved beyond the stage of childish crushes.'

It was a half-truth. She'd definitely moved beyond childish crushes. *But what about the more adult version?*

He hesitated, his eyes searching hers. 'Keely, if you want to move out I'll understand.'

'Move out?' Her eyes widened. 'Do you want me to move out?'

'Of course I don't. You're fantastic with Phoebe, even when she's at her most difficult, and you're helping me out of a very tight spot. I'd have to be mad to want to let you go. But you're making all the sacrifices.'

'I'm helping a friend,' she said gently, touching his arm. 'And I'll carry on helping for just as long as you need me. Now, are you going to relax and make us both some coffee or are you going to continue scowling at me?'

She busied herself tidying up the kitchen, hoping that he'd drop the subject. She didn't want to be forced to examine her feelings for him too closely. She had a feeling that what she might find would scare her even more than Zach.

The rest of the week passed quickly and on Friday Keely was snatching a well-deserved cup of coffee in the staff common room when Adam came into the room.

'OK, who's the best with screaming toddlers?' He flopped into one of the chairs and pulled a face. 'I've totally failed, I'm afraid. I can't get near the child.'

Nicky grinned. 'I thought you had children of your own.'

'I have.' Adam looked sheepish. 'My wife deals with the difficult bits. Tantrums are her department.'

Keely took pity on him and stood up. 'What's the story?'

'Head injury and, frankly, it's heading fast for another one if it doesn't stop flinging itself on the ground.'

'You'd probably strike up a better relationship if you didn't refer to the child as "it",' Keely said dryly, walking towards the door and looking towards Nicky. 'Any help on offer?'

'Zoe is already down in the paediatric area,' Nicky said hurriedly. 'And she's a qualified paediatric nurse. Much better with toddlers than I am.'

Keely glanced round at her colleagues in frustration. 'You're all hopeless!'

Rolling her eyes and shaking her head, she left the room and walked down the corridor, wincing as she heard the screams. Adam hadn't been exaggerating. The little girl was lying on the floor, ignoring all attempts to soothe and placate her.

Keely gave the A and E staff nurse a smile and walked casually over to the toy box. Then she sat down on the floor and started rummaging through it, careful not to look at the toddler.

'Oh, look at this, Zoe!' She pulled out a brightly coloured train and set it on the floor. 'Have we got any track?'

She rummaged again and managed to find some track.

'You start at that end of the room, Zoe, and I'll meet you in the middle.'

The staff nurse obligingly dropped to her knees and started to assemble the train track. As Keely had hoped, the screaming suddenly stopped and the toddler sat watching them, thumb jammed into her mouth.

'Any carriages?' Keely delved again and found a rather battered carriage. 'Perfect. Now I need someone to fix it to the engine.'

'Em's turn.' The child scrambled unevenly to her feet and tottered over. 'Em's turn.'

'Is that you?' Keely handed her the carriage. 'Are you Em?'

The toddler nodded, thumb still jammed in her mouth.

'Short for Emma—or Emily?'

'Emily,' the mother said quietly. 'But we tend to call her Em because that's what she calls herself.'

'And how old is she?'

'Two and a half.'

'Right.' Keely turned back to the toddler. 'What colour is this train, Em?'

'Wed. Wed and boo.'

'Clever girl.' Keely beamed at her. 'Red and blue. And can you fix it to the carriage for me?'

Em removed her thumb from her mouth and snapped the two toys together with ease.

'Brilliant. Now, can you put them on the track and push them to my friend Zoe?'

The toddler plopped onto the floor and pushed the train along to the nurse.

'Well, she seems quite lucid and she's playing happily,' Keely said, reaching for the notes Zoe had placed on the couch and quickly scanning them. 'What happened, Mrs Barrett?'

'She tripped and banged her head on the coffee-table.'

Was it her imagination or did the woman look nervous?

'And did she cry straight away?'

Mrs Barrett nodded and licked her lips. 'Oh, yes. She was hysterical.'

Keely gave her a sympathetic smile. 'Well, at least we know she wasn't knocked out. Has she been sick or drowsy?'

'No, nothing like that.'

'I just need to take a look in her eyes and examine

the bump,' Keely explained, reaching for an oph-thalmoscope and a teddy. 'OK, look at this, Em.'

She switched on the ophthalmoscope and pointed it at the teddy, pretending to examine its button eyes.

'Em's turn.' The toddler was by her side in an instant. 'Want torch.'

'Please,' her mother prompted automatically.

'Pees.' The little girl reached out to grab the oph-thalmoscope and Keely whipped out a pen torch. 'This one's for Em. Em, look at the teddy and Keely look at Em.'

Quickly, knowing that she didn't have time to waste, she examined the child's eyes.

'Does your head hurt, Em?'

'Em hurt. Rick push Em.'

Keely stopped what she was doing and her eyes met the mother's. 'Someone pushed her?'

'No.' Mrs Barrett swept the toddler into her arms. 'No one pushed her. My boyfriend was walking past and knocked into her, but it was an accident.'

Keely's instincts were on full alert but she knew better than to alienate the mother at this stage.

'That happens so easily with toddlers.' She held out her arms. 'Em come with Keely?'

Em slipped easily into her arms and she strolled up to the trolley and sat her down.

'I just need to finish examining her, Mrs Barrett.'

She slipped the little girl's dress over her head and tickled the child's stomach until she gurgled with laughter.

The mother stared at her suspiciously. 'Why are you undressing her when she banged her head?'

'Because toddlers fall for a number of reasons,' Keely said smoothly. 'Sometimes it's because they're unsteady on their feet and sometimes it could be because they have an infection of some sort which can affect their balance. We always do a full check with a head injury. I'll want to check her ears and throat as well.'

Zoe stepped over, her expression friendly. 'Mrs Barrett, can I just get you to fill out this card for me with Emily's details?'

As the child's mother followed Zoe without question, Keely was able to examine the child thoroughly, which had obviously been the staff nurse's intention. Blessing her quick thinking, Keely examined the child, frowning slightly as she saw the faint yellow bruises on her upper arms.

Her lower legs were covered in bruises, too, but these were less concerning because children of Emily's age fell over so frequently.

Taking a quick look at her back, she saw faint marks that made her feel decidedly uneasy. Could it be what she suspected? It was so difficult to tell in children of this age who were frequently covered in bruises.

'Well done, Em.' She slipped the dress back over the little girl's head and glanced at Zoe.

'I just need to talk to Mr Jordan and then we'll sort out that head.' She turned to the mother with a relaxed smile. 'Mrs Barrett, Emily has a nasty bump on the head and we may well need to admit her to our paediatric ward for twenty-four hours' observation.'

The mother looked uneasy. 'I thought she could go straight home.'

'I don't think so.' Keely wrote carefully on the notes, documenting everything she'd found. 'Head injuries can be deceptive in small children. I just need to talk to one of our consultants.'

She walked briskly down the corridor and found Zach examining a young woman with chest pains.

'Can I see you when you have a minute?'

He gave a nod, finished his examination and then handed over to Adam.

'Problems?' He walked with her into the corridor and she bit her lip.

'Maybe. I've got a two-and-a-half-year-old in Paediatric Casualty with a bang on the head. Mother says she tripped and banged her head on the table but the toddler says she was pushed. I've examined her thoroughly and she has marks consistent with old bruising on her upper arms and back.'

'Children of that age are always covered in bruises,' Zach reminded her, his gaze quizzical. 'Phoebe's the same.'

Keely nodded. 'I know that. But these bruises aren't in the common places.'

Zach rubbed his chin, his expression suddenly watchful. 'And you think it's non accidental?'

'I don't know.' Keely hesitated. 'I don't want to think that, but all my instincts are saying that something isn't right.'

'How does she react to the mother?'

'Fine.' Keely shrugged. 'Mother seems a bit nervous but that could just be because it's hospital, of course.'

'Any sign of Dad?'

Keely shook her head, wishing his gaze wasn't quite so blue or so direct. It made it hard to concentrate. 'No dad. Mother mentioned a boyfriend. The same person that the toddler said pushed her.'

Zach frowned. 'I don't think you can rely on the evidence of a two-and-a-half-year-old, Keely.'

Keely took a deep breath. 'I know that, but will you just look at her?'

'I'll look at her.' For a moment their eyes held and tension sparked between them, then he muttered something under his breath and strode off down the corridor, leaving her feeling weak-kneed.

Quickly she pulled herself together and caught up with him. 'I've warned the mother that we may want to admit her for twenty-four hours' observation.'

Zach paused. 'Have you checked the register?'

Keely shook her head. All the A and E staff had access to the Child Protection Register which listed children considered to be at risk.

'Check the register and meet me down there.'

Zach strode off and Keely hurried to Reception. There was no record of the child on the register, and by the time she got back to Paediatric Casualty Zach had finished his examination.

He was playing comfortably with Emily and had the mother eating out of his hand.

'Dr Thompson is quite right, Mrs Barrett,' he said smoothly, casting a relaxed smile in Keely's direction. Not by the flicker of an eyelid did he betray that anything was amiss. 'Emily has had a bang on the head so we would like to keep her in overnight. I'll call the paediatricians.'

Mrs Barrett complained a bit but also looked slightly relieved.

'Odd,' Keely said afterwards as she and Zach walked back towards the staffroom. 'It was almost as if she wanted the child to be admitted.'

'So maybe it is the boyfriend and he's out of control.' Zach shrugged and held the door open for her. 'Either way, it's not our problem any more. Paeds can deal with it. If necessary, they'll get an emergency protection order.'

Keely bit her lip. 'But maybe I should contact the community health nurse or the GP, or maybe—'

'Keely, this is A and E,' Zach pointed out gently. 'The child has been admitted. Paeds will deal with all that.'

'But—'

'We can't get involved in the small details of people's lives,' Zach reminded her. 'We just repair the surface damage and leave the rest to someone else.'

But that wasn't what she wanted to do. She wanted to see it through. She wanted to make sure that the patients were all right once they got home, that they could cope...

'Three cheers for Keely.' Adam was back in the common room, a big grin on his face. 'What you don't know, Dr Thompson, is that we all sneaked down after you to watch you with that child. We thought we might learn something.'

'Never knew you liked trains so much,' Nicky teased, 'or that you found the floor so comfortable.'

Keely rolled her eyes. 'Pick up any tips?'

'Yes.' Adam gave a broad grin. 'If it's a child, call Keely. I need all the help I can get when it comes to children. I'm the first to admit it. I never know where to start but you were fantastic.'

'You're being ridiculous,' Keely said gruffly, blushing as she walked across to the kettle and flicked the switch. 'I'm no better with children than anyone else is.'

'Yes, you are.' Zach looked at her steadily. 'Adam's right. You're incredibly good with children. You know just what to say and what to do to get the best out of them. You're great at averting tantrums and you seem to be able to coax a smile from the most moody, miserable child.'

She stared at him, stunned by his praise, and then Adam cleared his throat.

'So, on the strength of that reference, Dr Thompson, maybe you should be applying for a job as a paediatrician. What is it you're planning to do when you finish here?'

Keely licked dry lips. 'Cardiology.'

'Well, it's a waste,' Adam said cheerfully. 'You should definitely go into paediatrics. Don't you agree, Zach?'

There was a brief silence while Zach watched her. 'I think she should do whatever she wants to do.'

Keely turned away quickly and busied herself making the coffee. She wished they'd change the subject. She really didn't know what she wanted to do, or how she felt about her career.

She passed Zach a coffee and for a brief moment their eyes meshed. And she knew. Knew without a doubt that there was one thing she *was* sure of. She loved Zach Jordan.

She always had, and she always would.

CHAPTER FIVE

IT WAS her turn to cook supper.

Keely let herself into the house, said goodnight to Barbara, who'd been in charge all day, then played a game about body parts with a giggling Phoebe.

'Nose.' Phoebe put a little hand over her nose and then touched Keely's nose.

'Eyes.' Keely pointed to her eyes and then her chin. 'What's this?'

'Chin.' Phoebe clambered onto Keely's lap and buried her face in her chest. 'Bosoms. Nice. Soft.'

Keely's chuckle turned to a blush as she glanced up and saw Zach standing there. 'Oh!' her voice was an embarrassed squeak. 'We didn't hear you.'

He didn't even try and hide his laughter. 'Obviously not.'

Help! Why did he make her feel so hot and bothered? And why, when she was dying to see the man laugh, did it have to be at her expense?

'Well, now you're home you can take over and I'll make supper. You did it last night.' Keely stood up and handed him his daughter, her face still burning with mortification.

'Neck.' Phoebe reached out and wrapped her arms around her father's neck, and Keely slunk out of the room before the child picked out any more embarrassing bits. Next time she'd just play a quiet game of hide and seek.

She concentrated her attentions on the supper and by the time Zach reappeared, having put Phoebe to bed, she had herself under control again.

'Adam was right. You're so good with small children,' he observed, leaning forward and helping himself to some olives she'd put on the table.

Keely laughed and gave the casserole a stir. 'Don't tell me—you think I should be a paediatrician, too.'

He sat back in his chair. 'What I think doesn't matter—you should be what you want to be.' His tone was even. 'Why do you want to be a cardiologist?'

Her hand froze and for a moment she stopped stirring. The honest answer was that she didn't know that she *did* want to be a cardiologist. But she couldn't tell him that. Zach was like the rest of her family, ferociously intelligent and aiming for the top of his profession. He wouldn't understand her doubts. Wouldn't understand if she confessed that she wasn't sure she wanted any sort of hospital career...

'Why do I want to be a cardiologist?' She started stirring again and fished around in her brain for the sort of plausible answer one might give at an interview. 'All sorts of reasons. I find cardiology fascinating, I like the intellectual challenge, the variety, the research opportunities—loads of things.'

She tasted the casserole, added more salt and then placed it in the centre of the table.

'This smells delicious.' Zach leaned forward and

gave an appreciative sniff. 'So, have you applied for anything?'

'Not yet.' She handed him a spoon and watched while he served himself. 'There's a post coming up in London that Dad wants me to apply for. It's with Professor Harding.'

'*The* Professor Harding?' Zach lifted an eyebrow. 'I'm impressed. You're certainly heading for the big time.'

'I didn't say I'd got the post,' Keely reminded him dryly. 'I just said that Dad wants me to apply.'

Zach was suddenly still. 'And are you going to?'

'Probably,' Keely said quietly, carefully hiding just how unenthusiastic she felt about the whole thing. 'But he gets loads of applicants, of course, so I probably won't even get an interview.'

'You're a clever girl, Keely. I'm sure you'll walk into any job you want.' His jaw was tense. 'So you're definitely planning on going back to London at the end of your six months, then?'

His tone was slightly cool and she frowned slightly, wondering why. Was he checking that she wasn't getting any silly ideas about staying near him? That she wasn't altering her career plans for him? Well, he didn't need to worry on that score. Whatever she decided about her future, she was going to make sure it was well away from Zach. He'd made it crystal clear that he didn't want any sort of relationship with her. Or with any other woman.

She gave a nod. 'Yes, I'm going back to London.'

It would be the best thing for all of them. Obviously what he'd shared with his wife had been too special ever to be repeated. But everyone needed friends and she could be a good friend to him. She'd stay around and help him until he sorted out his child-care arrangements and then she'd move out and try to build a life without him.

The next day they were both working the early shift and it turned into a horrendously busy morning. The weather was freezing, the roads were icy and by nine o'clock they'd had two nasty RTAs—road traffic accidents—admitted to the unit.

They'd only just cleared up and restocked the resus room when a man was admitted with a penetrating chest injury.

'He was stabbed on his way to work. Would you believe it? Broad daylight. What a bloodbath,' Nicky muttered as she applied pressure to the wounds and jerked her head towards a nurse. 'Someone call Zach now! *Move!*'

'What happened?' Zach came into Resus seconds later, took one look at the patient and started scrubbing.

'He was stabbed twice in the chest.' Keely's voice faltered slightly as she struggled to get a line in. Thank goodness Zach was here. For once she was willing to admit that she was totally out of her depth. 'He's got distended neck veins, hypotension and muffled heart sounds. I think he might have a cardiac tamponade.'

A tamponade was bleeding into the sac that surrounded the heart and Keely knew it was potentially life-threatening.

Zach lathered down to his elbows. 'Has he got an output?'

'Yes—I've fast-bleeped the cardiothoracic team but they're in the Operating Theatre. They'll be here as soon as possible.'

'OK.' Zach turned the taps off with his elbows. 'Let's give him oxygen, Nicky, and get two lines in. And someone get me a thoracotomy tray just in case.'

'It's on your left,' Nicky said as she glanced at the monitor. 'Damn. He's arrested.'

'OK, we're going to have to open him up.' Zach spoke calmly, as if it were an everyday occurrence. 'Get that pack open, Nicky, and let's get some blood down here fast. I'm going to open his chest.'

He worked with such speed and skill that Keely couldn't keep pace with him.

'Rib retractors!'

Obediently Keely produced the retractors and helped him position them so that he had better access to the chest cavity.

'OK, I can see the heart. Hell, what a mess.' He frowned and reached into the chest while Keely watched in silent admiration. How could he begin to see what he was doing? With a sure movement he cut through the bulging pericardium and evacuated the blood. 'I can see a tear.'

He put his finger over the defect and performed internal cardiac massage by pressing the heart between his hands.

Just then the doors flew open and the cardiothoracic surgeon strode in. 'For Pete's sake, Zach, couldn't you wait?'

'Needed the practice.' Zach grinned and glanced towards Nicky. 'Get the expert some gloves, will you? And some 4/0 prolene sutures.'

Swiftly the team worked together to save the man, and finally Zach glanced up at the monitor. 'All right, I'm stopping massage.'

There was a tense silence in the room while everyone watched the monitor and then Zach muttered under his breath, 'Come on, come on, give me an output.'

As if following his instructions, the ECG machine sprang to life and Keely gasped with delight, as did the rest of the team.

'Good work, folks.' Zach glanced up. 'Let's get a CVP line in and give him some cefuroxime. Then I want an arterial line inserted and a catheter. Keely, recheck his U and E, glucose, FBC and clotting, please. Anything else, David?'

'You've just about covered it,' the cardiothoracic surgeon drawled, lifting an eyebrow. 'Are you after my job?'

'Most definitely not.' Zach stripped off his gloves and gave a wry smile. 'I can't stand the sight of blood.'

The immediate crisis over, Keely treated herself to a long look at Zach. His short hair was slightly dishevelled, his jaw was already showing signs of stubble and his eyes were beginning to show the strain of the past few hours. But she'd never loved him more in her life. Not just because he was so handsome that he made her knees weak, but because he was the cleverest, most impressive man she'd ever met.

Her siblings were clever, but somehow they always managed to make her feel inferior. Zach never did that. He made everyone feel that their contribution was important. And no matter what came through the doors, Zach never lost his cool. Even when he was operating under pressure, he still found time to involve and praise the staff who worked with him. He'd thanked them as a team for saving the young man's life, but in reality the skill had been *his*.

'Snap out of it.' Nicky's soft voice brought her back to earth sharply and Keely gave a weak smile.

'Sorry. I was dreaming.'

'And no prizes for guessing who you were dreaming about.' Nicky adjusted the IV and put the notes on the trolley, ready for transfer to the Intensive Therapy Unit. 'Mind you, I don't blame you. That was some performance. Impressive, isn't he?'

Keely nodded and glanced across the room to where Zach was standing with the cardiothoracic surgeon. 'How does he do it?' She kept her voice low so that he couldn't hear her. 'How can he stay so calm? All I could see was blood. Why didn't he panic?'

'Zach? Zach never panics,' Nicky said simply. 'Nothing ever throws him. Certainly not blood. But, then, he was a surgeon, of course. I suppose that helps.'

And he'd been a very skilled surgeon if her father's reports were correct.

'Well, that man was jolly lucky he was on duty,' Keely said gruffly, and Nicky gave her a sympathetic smile.

'Oh, dear, you really have got him badly, haven't you?'

Keely opened her mouth to deny it but then decided not to bother. 'Very badly. I can't sleep without dreaming of him and I lose concentration at work if I'm not very, very careful. I'm afraid I'm going to do myself serious internal damage hiding it from him.'

'Never mind that,' Nicky muttered hastily. 'Just make sure you *do* hide it or you'll find that he also has a reputation for biting impatience with women who drool over him.'

Keely bit her lip and then gave a start as she realised that he'd walked over to her, his blue eyes quizzical.

'Is something wrong?' His voice was quiet.

'Yes. I'm feeling totally incompetent,' she confessed, sliding her fingers through her blonde hair and giving a helpless shrug. 'I was useless back there and I'm really sorry.'

'Useless?' He looked genuinely puzzled. 'When were you useless?'

'With that patient. I didn't have a clue what to do, and I couldn't keep up with you—'

'Keely, the man was stabbed through the heart. I wouldn't have expected you to know what to do.' He frowned and shook his head slightly. 'That sort of emergency happens about once every year or even less in A and E. It's almost impossible to gain experience in that sort of technique.'

'But you knew what to do, Zach.'

And from what she'd seen, he *always* knew what to do.

'I'm a consultant, Keely,' he reminded her gently. 'I'm supposed to know what to do. In another seven years you'll know what to do as well if you choose to stay in this discipline. Don't lose confidence. You're an excellent doctor.'

'Oh.' She blushed slightly, warmed by his praise. 'Had you done that before?'

'Several times.' He gave a wry smile. 'I worked in South Africa for a while and there's no shortage of trauma experience there, I can assure you.'

He stepped to one side to have a final word with the cardiothoracic surgeon, and Keely dragged her eyes away from him with a huge effort.

'Keely, you're doing it again,' Nicky muttered in an undertone. 'Get a grip.'

'Sorry.'

She couldn't help the way she felt about him. She loved him more every day and she loved Phoebe, too. And the more she loved them, the more she wanted to make everything better for them.

Arriving at work the next morning, Keely wondered how much longer she was going to be able to carry on working with Zach without giving herself away. Every time he walked into the room her knees wobbled alarmingly and her pulse rate soared.

At least the department was busy, which helped take her mind off him for some of the time.

She was seeing a woman with an injured wrist when she heard screaming from Resus.

Now what?

Even as she was wondering what was happening one of the student nurses appeared at her elbow.

'Can you come quickly, Dr Thompson?'

Immediately Keely excused herself and hurried into Resus.

'What's the problem?'

'Help!' A young woman was sobbing and yelling, her white-faced husband clutching her hand as she writhed on the trolley.

'How are you at delivering babies?' Nicky asked grimly, wrenching open a delivery pack and addressing the student nurse. 'Call the labour ward now, please—get them down here urgently. Zach's on his way.'

Delivering babies?

Keely felt a twinge of panic. She hadn't done obstetrics yet and although she'd seen a baby delivered as a medical student, she was hardly an expert.

'When's the baby due?'

The woman groaned but her husband glanced up, his face strained. 'Not for another week.'

'And is this your first baby?'

He nodded. 'Yes. I thought first labours were supposed to last a long time.'

'Not always,' Keely murmured, giving them a reassuring smile. 'But don't worry. Everything will be fine. OK.' She took a deep breath. 'Can I have some size-six gloves, please, Nicky, and let's listen to the foetal heart.'

She was washing her hands when Zach arrived, his eyes focusing straight on Keely.

'What's the story?'

'Precipitate labour,' Keely said quickly, relief flooding through her. At least the responsibility wasn't all hers now. Would Zach know what to do?

He did, of course, dragging on a pair of sterile gloves and examining the labouring woman, talking quietly to her all the time.

His voice seemed to calm her and the woman stopped screaming, instead tightening her grip on her husband's hand and fastening her eyes on Zach with a trusting expression on her face.

'It's coming, isn't it?'

'It certainly is.' Zach gave a lopsided grin and then glanced at the notes to check the woman's name. 'Try and remember your breathing, Tina. That's it— good.' He looked at Nicky. 'Let's give her some Entonox, please. Keely? Do you want to…?'

He was asking her if she wanted to deliver the baby and she shook her head vigorously. She didn't have the confidence to deliver a baby.

'No—no, you do it.'

He gave a slight smile and stood on the right of the patient. 'OK, Tina, just keep breathing, that's it…'

'I've rung the labour ward,' Nicky said in an undertone, 'and someone is coming down to help.'

'Well, they're not going to be much help unless they're here in the next two minutes,' Zach said calmly, 'because this baby isn't going to wait. All right, Tina, you're doing well. I can see the baby's head. Let's see if we can get you a bit more upright.'

They helped Tina wriggle into a better position and Zach waited until her next contraction.

'Keely, come a bit closer so that you can see.'

Keely obeyed his instruction, watching with fascination as the baby's head crowned.

'The foetal heart is dipping,' Nicky said quietly, and Zach nodded.

'Pant for me, Tina,' he said quietly. 'Don't push. Good girl, well done. Let's get this baby out.'

Keely watched as he used his left hand to control the rate of escape of the head.

'Excellent.' Having delivered the head, he allowed it to extend and then used his fingers to feel for the cord, slipping it over the baby's neck. 'There we are. Nicky, have you got the ergometrine ready?' He turned back to Tina. 'We're just going to give you something to make your uterus contract once the baby is delivered. It's perfectly normal.'

She nodded and then screwed up her face and yelled as another contraction hit her and the baby shot into Zach's waiting hands.

He placed the baby gently on Tina's stomach. 'A little girl. Congratulations.'

'Oh, Mike!' Tina looked at her husband and tears spilled down her cheeks. 'Mike, she's beautiful.'

'She certainly is.' Her husband bent down and kissed her gently, his eyes damp. 'We're a family now. A real family.'

The baby cried loudly and everyone sniffed and

looked decidedly emotional. All except Zach, whose face was strangely devoid of expression.

Keely watched as he clamped the cord and cut it and then examined the vessels.

Something was the matter with him.

Was it seeing the baby born? Was it the husband's comments about being a family? It must be awful for him, seeing other happy couples with children when he—

Damn. She couldn't bear to think about how much he must be hurting.

'Keely.' His voice was slightly sharp, as if he'd guessed what she was thinking. 'Can you remember what to look for?' He was as cool and professional as ever as she moved closer to see what he was doing.

'Two arteries?'

'That's right.' He shifted his position just as a man in theatre greens walked into the room.

Zach looked up. 'You've missed the action, Jed. Sorry.'

The other man grinned and looked down at the woman on the trolley. 'Trying to give everyone a heart attack, were you, Tina?'

The young woman still looked shell-shocked. 'At least she didn't arrive while we were shopping.'

'Yes, let's be thankful for small mercies,' the obstetrician agreed, glancing at Zach. 'Any problems?'

Zach shook his head. 'I'm just delivering the placenta. Do you want to take over?'

'Not especially.' But Jed stayed close by, talking

calmly to the couple, keeping an eye on proceedings. Finally he gave Zach a thump on the back.

'Well done. We'll take it from here if that's all right with you.'

'Fine.' Zach stood up and ripped off his gloves, tossing them in the bin before moving back to the trolley and smiling at Tina. 'Well done.'

'You can have a cuddle if you like,' Tina said, but Zach's smile faded and his expression was suddenly remote.

'Thanks, but I'd better not. The sooner you get up to the ward the better.'

With that he picked up the notes and glanced at Nicky. 'I'll write up the notes in my office. Can one of you take them up to the ward later?'

Nicky nodded. 'Of course.'

Keely watched with concern as he strode out of the room. He was upset. He was definitely upset.

So what should she do about it?

Should she ignore it? Let him bottle it up?

Or should she follow her instincts and see if he needed a friend...?

CHAPTER SIX

KEELY hesitated outside Zach's office and then tapped gently on the door.

He should have finished writing the notes by now but there was no sign of him emerging from his office. And she was worried about him.

She tapped again and gingerly opened the door, stopping dead when she saw him standing with his back to her, his powerful shoulders tense as he stared out of the window at the snow-capped mountains.

'Zach?'

He didn't turn. 'The notes are on the desk.'

Keely closed the door behind her, refusing to be daunted by his discouraging tone.

'I don't want the notes.' On impulse she turned the key in his door and then stood for a moment, wondering how best to break down the barriers he'd built around himself.

He turned to face her, his eyes tired. 'This isn't a good time.'

'I know that.' She hesitated, knotting her fingers together anxiously. 'But I was worried about you'

'I'm fine, Keely.' He looked at her for a moment and then turned back to the window. 'And I need to be on my own.'

She ought to be taking the hint and leaving him to his own thoughts, however painful, but she sensed how much he was hurting and couldn't leave him alone.

'Please.' Her voice was soft. 'I want to help, Zach.'

'How?' He gave a harsh laugh. 'No one can help. Not even you.'

Keely felt her heart twist. There must be *something* she could do—surely just knowing that someone cared must help a little bit?

She closed the gap between them until she was standing so close they were almost touching.

His dark jaw was tense. 'I really don't want to talk about this.'

'Well, you should,' she said bravely, ignoring his curt tone. 'You told me that if things upset me here, I should talk to you. I think it's time you followed some of your own advice, Zach. Tell me why you're upset. Talk to me. Was it the baby being born?'

He swore fluently under his breath and his blue gaze was menacing. 'Keely, I *don't* need to talk. I don't *want* to talk.'

His words throbbed with pain and on impulse she stood on tiptoe and hugged him, the same way she would have hugged Phoebe if she'd been upset.

Standing rigid in her embrace, Zach lifted his hands and gripped her arms tightly, clearly intending to remove them.

'For God's sake, Keely.'

His words were like a shower of cold water.

What on earth was she doing?

'I'm sorry.' She stepped back, mortified, realising that he'd misinterpreted her actions. Bother. It had been a simple hug. Nothing more. But he'd thought... He'd obviously assumed...

She closed her eyes, thoroughly confused and embarrassed. Now what?

'I'm sorry, Zach,' she mumbled finally, not quite meeting his eyes. 'I was just trying to help. I wasn't. Oh, damn.'

'Hush...'

She felt his hands on her shoulders and glanced up awkwardly, preparing herself to apologise again—to explain that she hadn't been throwing herself at him. Instead, the words died in her throat and what she saw in his eyes took her breath away.

'Keely.' He said her name softly, his strong fingers stroking through her blonde hair as he scanned every inch of her face. 'Little Keely. You can't see anyone hurt and not try and help, can you?'

'I'm not little.' She frowned, hurt that he seemed to be dismissing her concern so lightly. 'I'm an adult, remember? I don't—'

'Dammit, I know you're an adult.' He growled the words against her mouth and then suddenly he was kissing her. Kissing her the way he'd kissed her that night in Phoebe's bedroom.

She gave a soft gasp and he took instant advantage, steadying her head with strong hands as he deepened the kiss.

Her heart thudding erratically, she melted into him and with a rough exclamation his arms slid round her, trapping her against his powerful body.

Swamped with need, her knees sagged and without breaking the kiss he propelled her backwards until her shoulders came into contact with the wall, his body hard against hers as he continued to drive them both to a frenzy of need. He seemed to know exactly how to kiss her, exactly what to do to excite her the most.

His breathing harsh, he lifted her skirt, his hands sliding up the warmth of her trembling thighs and cupping her bottom.

'Dear God, Keely…' He muttered the words against her mouth, his strong fingers tightening on her flesh, his touch sending rivers of wild excitement tumbling through her insides.

'Zach…' She was trembling like a leaf in a storm, her whole body consumed by the fire he'd ignited inside her. She felt his fingers tugging at her skimpy pants and gave a soft gasp as he sought access to the very heart of her passion.

She clutched his shoulders and her breath came in tiny pants as her body responded to the touch of his clever fingers. She couldn't believe what was happening, couldn't understand the response that he coaxed from her, and she trembled as she felt the ripples of sensation spread through her body. For a brief moment in time she forgot where she was—she forgot *who* she was—aware only of the sudden explosion within her body. His mouth captured her cries of ecstasy and afterwards she nestled against him, hiding her burning face in the cool fabric of his shirt.

'Oh, Zach…' She whispered his name, not daring to look at him. 'I wasn't— I didn't mean to—'

He gave a soft laugh, his warm breath brushing

the top of her head. 'You didn't. I did. If anyone needs to apologise here, it's me.'

She shook her head, her cheeks still burning. *How could she have let him do that? How could she have been so totally shameless?*

'Keely, look at me.'

She ignored his quiet command, her face still buried in his shirt.

'I can't. I'm too embarrassed.'

With a soft curse he slipped a hand under her chin and lifted her face so that she was forced to look at him.

'Zach, I really didn't mean…' She swallowed hard and tried again. 'I don't want you to think— When I hugged you, I wasn't throwing myself at you.'

'I know that.' A ghost of a smile played around his firm mouth. 'You were trying to comfort me, and I'm sorry.'

Her eyes widened. 'Why are *you* sorry?'

'Because I was the one who kissed you. And I shouldn't have done it.' He hesitated and then gave a humourless laugh. 'I always seem to be saying that to you, don't I?'

Keely closed her eyes, still hideously embarrassed. 'Zach, it was my fault, not yours—'

Zach covered her lips with a gentle finger, stopping her in mid-flow. 'It wasn't anyone's fault, Keely. The truth is that you and I can't seem to be within a metre of each other without sparking enough electricity to power the whole of the national grid.' His hand dropped and suddenly he looked weary. 'But it doesn't change the fact that I have nothing to offer any woman at the moment. The truth is that after Catherine I haven't got anything left to give anyone.'

'I know. I understand. Truly I do.' With a massive effort Keely flashed him a smile. 'Let's just forget it. It was just a kiss.'

The way he lifted an eyebrow made her realise how totally ridiculous it was to refer to what they'd shared as 'just a kiss'.

Saying that it was 'just a kiss', was like saying that Everest was just a mountain!

'What I mean,' she said hastily, 'is that you don't need to worry that I'll read anything into it—you know that all I'm interested in at the moment is my career. I'm certainly not looking for permanent attachments. It won't be long before I'm off to London to start a new job.'

Heavens, how could she tell such a lie and sound convincing?

'That's right, so you are.'

His manner suddenly cool, he turned and walked over to his desk, flicking open the notes and scanning them quickly.

Keely felt suddenly confused.

Now what had she said?

Surely her words should have reassured him?

She frowned, but before she could question him there was a tap on the door and Keely bit back a growl of frustration. Talk about rotten timing!

Zach strode across his office and opened the door, his manner as calm and unperturbed as always.

'Oh, Nicky, you want the notes.' Not by a tremor

of his voice did he betray the fact that only a minute or two earlier he and Keely had been locked together with a passion that had nearly singed the paint from the walls. 'Keely's ahead of you. I was just finishing them off.'

'OK.' Nicky gave them a cheerful smile. 'Wasn't it great to have the chance to deliver a baby? It's nice to have something cheerful happening in the department for a change, don't you think?'

'Wonderful.' Zach's tone was even but Keely could see that the tension was back and she wanted to scream with frustration. For a brief moment she'd broken down those barriers that he'd built around himself. He'd let her close to him.

He walked back to his desk, signed the notes and handed them to Keely.

'There we are—all yours.'

His glance was cool and professional, and she sagged with disappointment. What had happened to the passion that had exploded between them? He was so distant that their kiss might never have happened, but she knew that for those few wild moments he'd wanted her as much as she'd wanted him.

But now he'd had time to think, he was backing off again. The death of his wife had hurt him so badly that part of him couldn't let go—couldn't allow him to give himself to a woman again.

The rest of Keely's shift was a nightmare. Every time she looked at Zach she remembered his mouth on hers and his hands touching her body.

Several times he had to repeat instructions, and by

the end of the shift she was so jumpy that she thought everyone must have noticed that something was wrong.

She was relieved to climb into her little car, relieved to put some distance between her and Zach. Although not for long, of course. As they were both off duty he'd be under her nose tonight and the whole of tomorrow.

Torture.

When she arrived home she left a note on the kitchen table saying that she needed to get on with some studying and had taken her supper upstairs. At least that way she wouldn't have to spend an evening trying to pretend that she was totally indifferent to the man.

It was all very well telling herself that she wasn't going to throw herself at him, but it was becoming harder, not easier. She couldn't look at him without remembering how it had felt when he'd kissed her, and as for the rest…

She gave a groan and reached for a cardiology textbook. Maybe work would take her mind off Zachary Jordan.

Fortunately it snowed overnight, which at least provided a topic of conversation at the breakfast table.

'Good morning.' Zach strolled into the room and Keely's hands started to shake so badly that she dropped the packet of oats onto the floor.

Bother. Bother. Bother.

Why did he have such a powerful effect on her? And why did he have to look so good in the morning? One glance in the mirror had been enough to confirm that a sleepless night had done nothing for her own appearance. Her cheeks were pale and her blue eyes were shadowed. Obviously he hadn't suffered a similar fate, she thought dryly, noting how sleek and handsome he looked. But, then, why should he? From his point of view all they'd shared had been a kiss. A very memorable kiss, of course, but nothing that was going to disturb his sleep.

Nothing that came close to what he'd shared with his wife.

'Something wrong, Keely?' One dark eyebrow lifted and she gave a bright smile.

'Nothing at all,' she said as she stooped to retrieve the box of oats. 'Just a little tired. I was reading until very late.'

'Yes. I saw your note.' He poured himself some coffee and gave her a cool smile. 'What were you working on? Anything in particular?'

'I was looking through my cardiology textbook,' she told him, skimming over the fact that she'd barely taken in anything she'd read. Her mind had been well and truly on other things. Him.

'Were you preparing for your interview?'

'Yes.' She made some porridge for Phoebe, careful not to look at Zach. If she didn't look at him she could pretend he wasn't there. And then maybe she'd stop shaking.

Zach glanced out of the window and sipped his coffee. 'There's snow on the hills. How do you fancy taking Phoebe sledding?'

'Yes, yes.' Phoebe bounced happily in her chair. 'Phoebe sledding.'

Sledding.

In the snow.

Snow was cold. If things became too desperate maybe she could push some down the neck of her anorak to cool herself down.

'Good idea.'

She served the porridge, made herself a piece of toast—which she didn't touch—and then busied herself getting things ready for their outing.

By the time they were ready to leave she had Phoebe warmly dressed in an all-in-one skisuit and furry boots.

Zach left his car by the side of the road and the three of them scrambled up the side of the mountain until they reached a suitable slope.

'Nice.' Phoebe bent down and tapped the snow with her mitten and then plopped down onto her bottom. 'Phoebe slide.'

'Wait.' Zach laughed and lifted her onto the sled before climbing on himself and holding onto the ropes. 'OK, off we go.'

They shot down the slope, Phoebe whooping with delight, and Keely watched with a smile and a lump in her throat.

Oh, she loved them both so much.

Then Zach dragged the sled back up the hill and it was her turn. She settled herself behind the little girl, held her tightly and then shot down the slope so fast that she gasped with fright.

The sled hit a bump and they both tumbled off into a pile of soft snow.

'More. More.' Phoebe bounced up immediately, totally undaunted by the crash, but Keely lay still for a minute, slightly winded.

'Are you all right?' Zach strode down the slope, scooped his daughter into his arms and then held out a hand to Keely. 'Come on.'

He hauled her upright and she stumbled against him, feeling the hard muscles of his thighs pressing against her.

For a moment their eyes locked and she knew that he was remembering their kiss. Then his jaw seemed to tense and he released her, swinging Phoebe onto his shoulders and jogging back up the slope with her, leaving Keely to drag the sled after them.

Desperate to relieve the tension between them, Keely bent down and scooped up an armful of freezing snow and then crept up behind Zach, raised her right arm and aimed the ball of snow with deadly accuracy.

It hit his body with a satisfying, muted thump and he turned, his eyes gleaming as he prepared himself to retaliate.

'Keely, Keely—you really shouldn't have done that.' He was laughing now and she gave a shriek as he lowered Phoebe to the ground and bent to pick up some snow to throw.

'Phoebe, save me!' Keely turned and ran as fast as she could in her cumbersome boots, but he caught her easily, stuffing the snow down the neck of her jacket while she shrieked for mercy.

Phoebe joined in, dancing around with excitement, and soon it was all-out war. By the time they eventually arrived home, all three of them were soaked and laughing.

'You two go and have a shower and I'll make us some hot soup.' Keely walked through to the kitchen, rubbing her damp hair with a towel.

'That was fun.' Zach followed her into the kitchen and dropped their wet things on the floor. 'I haven't seen Phoebe laugh that much for ages. Thanks, Keely.'

'You're very welcome,' she said quietly, rummaging in the cupboard for some cans of soup. 'I had fun, too.'

It was true. She'd really enjoyed herself. She'd even managed to stop thinking about how much she loved Zach for five minutes.

She straightened and met his eyes, and for a moment they stared at each other, tension shimmering between them.

'Keely…' When Zach finally managed to find his voice it sounded gruff, as if his emotions were lodged in his throat.

'Daddy, Daddy—boots stuck.'

Phoebe's shout from the hall interrupted whatever he'd been about to say and he gave a sigh and closed his eyes briefly.

'OK. I'm coming, sweetheart.' He dragged his eyes away from Keely's with a visible effort and walked out of the room to see to his daughter.

Keely dropped onto a chair, feeling as though she'd been caught in the path of a tornado. She felt sure now that he *did* feel something for her, even if it was just a physical thing. But he clearly didn't intend to do anything about it. He was still in love with his wife and he wasn't ready to move on.

It continued to snow and the weather played havoc with the workload of the casualty department.

'Why don't people just stay indoors?' Nicky muttered as she looked at the ever-growing number of people in the waiting room. 'I've lost count of the number of people who have slipped on the ice today. Why don't they just stay in bed?'

The mere mention of bed made Keely think of Zach and brought a hot colour to her cheeks.

Nicky gave her an odd look. 'Are you all right? You're very red all of a sudden—maybe you're catching something.'

'I'm fine,' Keely said quickly, knowing that she'd already caught something. The trouble was, it was called Zach and, as far as she could tell, it was totally incurable. The only answer was work. 'I'd better get going. Do you want me to see the lady that the ambulance crew brought in last?'

Before Nicky could question her further she picked up a set of notes and made her way to one of the cubicles.

A white-haired lady was lying on the trolley covered in a blanket and a younger woman was hovering anxiously by her side.

'Hello, Mrs Weston. I'm Dr Thompson.' Keely introduced herself and then questioned them both about the injury.

'I was only going to the corner shop for a loaf,' the old lady fretted, and her daughter gave a long-suffering sigh.

'And I would have got that for you, Mum,' she said briskly, rolling her eyes at Keely. 'There was absolutely no need for you to go out at all today.'

'But I wanted to get out, dear,' her mother said placidly. 'If I don't get out, how will I keep these old joints of mine moving?'

The daughter opened her mouth to state the obvious, but caught Keely's look and decided to bite her tongue.

'You're right to try and get some exercise,' Keely said tactfully, examining her carefully, 'but I suppose in future it might be wiser to wait until the pavements aren't so slippery.'

The old lady gave a slight smile. 'Shall I tell you something, dear? It isn't always much fun being wise. Sometimes it's a better idea to just be reckless.'

'Mum!' Her daughter looked horrified but Keely returned the smile that Mrs Weston was giving her.

'You may be right,' she said softly, thinking about Zach. 'You never know what life is going to throw at you, so it's best to live life to the full while you can.'

Her examination revealed that the injured leg was shortened and externally rotated.

'You've fractured your hip, Mrs Weston,' she said quietly, and the daughter tutted.

'Oh, Mum!'

The old lady looked at Keely. 'So what happens now?'

'Well, I'll arrange for you to have a series of

X-rays, take some bloods and do a trace of your heart, and then I'm going to refer you to the ortho-paedic team because they're the experts. Would you like something for the pain, Mrs Weston?'

'Yes, please. If it's not too much trouble.'

'It's no trouble,' Keely assured her quickly, pop-ping her head around the door of the cubicle to look for Nicky. 'I just need to find a nurse and then we'll give you something.'

She found Nicky, arranged for her to give Mrs Weston something for the pain and then completed the X-ray request form.

No sooner had the old lady been transferred to the ward than another victim of the icy roads was rushed in by ambulance.

This time Zach took charge and there was no doubt in anyone's mind that the young motorcyclist was badly injured. His leathers were badly torn and he was obviously in severe pain.

'OK, let's get his leathers off and see what we've got.' Zach was his usual cool, professional self and Keely found it hard to believe that this was the same man who could kiss a woman senseless. It was as if there were two completely different sides to him. The trouble was, she loved them both. 'Let's give him oxygen and get a line in, please—we need U and Es, FBC and blood sugar, and cross-match four units of blood.'

With the severity of injury it was highly probable that the man was going to need a blood transfusion.

Keely inserted a large-bore intravenous cannula and attached it to an infusion of saline.

Zach glanced up from his examination. 'I'm going to do a femoral nerve block to relieve the pain.'

Anticipating his request, the A and E nurse passed him a 21-gauge needle with syringe and Keely watched while Zach palpated the femoral artery and then inserted the femoral nerve block.

'Right, let's sort out this traction—it'll help his pain and his blood loss and make it easier to move him to X-Ray.'

The A and E team splinted the man's leg, checked the pulses in his foot and then transferred him to the orthopaedic team.

'I'm jolly glad I'm not in the orthopaedic team today,' Keely muttered as she helped clear up the mess in Resus. 'They haven't had a moment to breathe since we started work.'

'You should see the fracture clinic,' Nicky agreed, attaching a giving set to a bag of saline in preparation for the next emergency to be brought through the doors. 'I've lost count of the number of Colles' fractures they've seen today. Why do people always put their hands out when they slip?'

'Well, it's either that or they bang their heads,' Zach pointed out dryly, tossing his gloves in the bin. 'They've got to fall on something. At least the wrist is neat and relatively quick to deal with.'

There followed a light-hearted conversation about which bits of the body each of them would like to break most or least and then they were all called away again to deal with a head injury.

By the time Keely arrived home she was totally

exhausted and she flopped onto Phoebe's bedroom floor to read her a story.

'Keekee poorly.' Phoebe stroked her head gently and Keely grinned up at her.

'I'm not poorly, minx. I'm just totally exhausted. Partly because thinking about your gorgeous daddy keeps me awake at night and partly because of my job, which wears me out during the day.'

She gave a groan, kicked off her shoes and stretched out on the cushions. 'Right. Which book are we having?'

Phoebe plodded over to her bookcase, stared at the contents and then tugged out a book, sending a shower of other books tumbling over the cheerful blue carpet.

Keely gave a groan but was too exhausted to get up and put all the books back. There was always tomorrow. Instead, she held out her hand and took the book from the mischievous toddler, snuggling the little girl into her lap.

'Mmm, you smell good,' she murmured, burying her face in the blonde hair and breathing in deeply. 'You smell of baths and babies and nice things like that.'

Phoebe frowned and pushed the book into her chest. 'Read,' she said firmly, and Keely saluted quickly.

'Yes, boss.'

She opened the book and started to read, totally absorbed in the wonderful pictures and the clever rhymes.

By the time she'd finished the book Phoebe was yawning, and Keely lifted her up and put her in the cot.

'There we are. Night-night.'

'Tuck me in,' Phoebe pleaded, her eyes huge, and Keely smiled.

'You want me to tuck you in? Of course. Lie down.'

But instead of lying down Phoebe slid her chubby arms round Keely's neck and squeezed.

'Want cuggle.'

'Cuddle. Of course you can have a cuddle.' She lifted the child out of her cot again, loving the way the little legs wound round her waist like honeysuckle. After a few minutes she gave Phoebe a final squeeze and tried to put her back in her cot, but she was having nothing of it.

'More cuggle.'

'Time for sleep now,' Keely said gently, trying to peel her away from her body, but Phoebe's grip tightened.

'No sleep. Cuggle Keekee. Sleep with Keekee.'

Oh, dear.

Keely was just pondering how to handle the situation when Zach appeared in the doorway, his top button undone and his jacket slung casually over one shoulder.

'Problems?'

He looked so wickedly handsome that she nearly dropped Phoebe and fell to the floor at his feet.

'She—she just wanted an extra cuddle.'

That sexy mouth, the same mouth that was capable

of doing such amazing things to her, curved into a smile.

'And who can blame her?' His eyes met hers briefly and then he turned his attention to his daughter.

'Phoebe come to Daddy.'

'No.' Phoebe's arms tightened around Keely's neck until she felt as though she were trapped in a vice. 'Stay with Keekee.'

Help! Now what? Inspiration struck and she tossed a book that she'd seen earlier into the cot. 'Phoebe, look!' She injected an enormous amount of excitement into her voice. 'Look what's waiting for you in the cot.'

As she'd hoped, the toddler turned, her attention caught by Keely's tone of voice, and she allowed herself to be lifted into the cot.

'Phew.' Keely grinned at Zach. 'For a moment there I thought I'd be sleeping in a cot tonight.'

Zach didn't laugh. Instead, his eyes were fixed on his daughter.

Keely's heart sank as she looked at his tense features. She could read his mind. He was worried that Phoebe was getting too attached to her.

'Go and get changed,' she said quickly, hoping to distract him. 'I'll pour us both a drink.'

He stood frozen to the spot, his eyes still fixed on his daughter, but then he gave a brief nod and turned on his heel, leaving her with a sinking heart.

In the kitchen she tugged open the fridge, poured them both a glass of wine and walked through to the sitting room. Zach had already lit a fire and it crackled and whispered in the hearth, sending a warm glow across the cosy room.

'Is that for me?' He walked up to her and took the wine with a nod of thanks and then strolled over to the fire.

'Zach?' She said his name tentatively, not sure how to broach the subject. 'Look, I know what you're thinking...'

'Do you?' He stared down into his wineglass, unsmiling. 'And what am I thinking?'

She swallowed hard. 'That Phoebe is getting too attached to me.'

There was a long silence and then he gave a short laugh. 'How come you're so good at reading my mind?'

Because I love you, she wanted to say, but managed to stop herself in time.

'I suppose it's a fairly obvious concern,' she said quietly, 'but I'm not going to hurt her, Zach.'

'No? As you rightly said, you're getting close to her. I've never seen her respond to anyone the way she responds to you. What happens when you leave?' His gaze was direct. 'What happens when you take up this cardiology job you keep talking about?'

The cardiology job she wasn't even sure she wanted...

'Well, I'll stay in touch,' she said lamely, and he gave a long sigh and picked up his wine again.

'Try explaining that to a three-year-old.'

This was ridiculous. She didn't want to go anywhere. She wanted to stay with both of them. But there was no way she was telling him that. There was no way she was throwing herself at him again.

'Look, Zach—'

'Forget it, Keely.' His voice was rough. 'It isn't your problem. It's mine. I need to work out what to do for the best. Maybe you moving in wasn't such a good idea after all.'

Her heart thudded heavily in her chest. 'Are you saying you want me to move out?'

She held her breath as she waited for his answer, her fingers coiling into her palms. She couldn't bear to move out.

He stared into the fire, his expression remote. 'No. I'm not saying that. At least, not yet. I'm hoping I can think of another solution.'

She could think of another solution.

Instead of asking her to leave, he could ask her to stay.

But Zach would never do that. He'd loved his wife too much to make a commitment to another woman.

CHAPTER SEVEN

As KEELY walked towards the staffroom the following Monday, Zach waylaid her.

'We've had a dinner invitation,' he said briefly. 'Sean and his wife have invited us over tonight.'

She swallowed. She had to spend a whole evening in Zach's company in front of other people? She'd never be able to do it without giving herself away.

She searched her brain for an excuse.

'Why don't I look after Phoebe for you?'

'She'll come, too.' Zach gave a tired smile and jammed his hands in his pockets. 'I probably ought to warn you that Sean's wife, Ally, is not particularly subtle when it comes to matchmaking attempts. And that's probably what this is. She's heard that you've moved in with me and she's hearing wedding bells.'

The woman obviously had a hearing problem, Keely thought wryly. There were certainly no bells ringing anywhere near Zach. Except maybe alarm bells.

'Right.' Keely gave him an awkward smile, not sure what to say. 'In that case, perhaps it would be best if I didn't come.'

'You've got to come,' Zach said dryly, 'or she'll smell a rat. Our only hope of escaping her well-meaning tendency to pair me up is to prove to her that we find each other totally resistible.'

And how on earth was she going to do that?

'OK.' She smiled with more conviction than she was feeling. 'Well, I'll just talk about going to London. That should convince them.'

'Yes. It certainly should.' Zach's smile faded and he glanced at his watch. 'I'll tell them we'll see them at seven, then.'

Keely watched him move down the corridor away from her and wondered how on earth she was going to spend a whole evening pretending to be indifferent to Zach.

It was a long and difficult day in A and E and by the time she got home she was totally drained. Goodness only knew how Zach would be feeling— he'd born the brunt of the trauma and tragedy they'd had to deal with in just one shift.

The last thing she really felt like doing was going out to dinner, but she didn't see how she could refuse.

She had a quick shower, applied some make-up to hide just how tired she was and on impulse ran Zach a bath.

He arrived home an hour after her with only twenty minutes to spare before they had to leave.

'What a day.' He shrugged his coat off and tossed it over the bannister before taking the stairs two at a time to the bathroom. 'You ran me a bath?'

He frowned and then glanced at her, and she blushed.

Hmm. Maybe she shouldn't have done that. On reflection it had been rather a wifely gesture, but at the time she'd thought it might help relax him after a hard day.

'You don't have to have it,' she said quickly, stroking her hair behind her ear as she always did when she was nervous. 'I just thought you'd had an awful day and I—'

'Hush. Stop apologising.' He put a finger over her lips and gave her a lopsided smile. 'It was a really sweet thought. I just keep forgetting what a truly nice person you are. Give me ten minutes to shave and change and I'll meet you downstairs.'

He was as good as his word and by the time she'd packed a small bag for Phoebe he was ready.

'OK. I'll just get the wine from the fridge…' He went through to the kitchen and came back holding two bottles. 'You take these and I can carry Phoebe.'

Keely risked a glance at him and then wished she hadn't. He was wearing a black poloneck jumper that emphasised the breadth of his shoulders and a pair of trousers that clung lovingly to his hard thighs. As usual he looked so handsome he took her breath away and she turned away quickly, sure that what she felt must show in her eyes.

They arrived at Sean's just after seven and Keely was immediately absorbed into the noise and warmth of the Nicholson household.

'Come on in and make yourselves comfortable.' Ally had a baby cuddled against her shoulder and a toddler tugging at her leg. 'For goodness' sake, Katy, Mummy's going to trip over you—Sean, I need a hand!'

Sean quickly swept the toddler into his arms, casting a rueful smile at Zach.

'Sorry. It's utter chaos here as usual. They're all meant to be in bed but they wanted to stay up and see you.'

'Don't apologise—we've brought one of our own,' Zach reminded them dryly, shifting Phoebe more comfortably in his arms.

'Why don't you men settle the children while Keely and I make some drinks?' Ally suggested, handing the baby over to Sean. 'Come on, Keely. I'll show you around.'

After Zach's warning, Keely was nervous about what Ally was going to say to her but she dutifully followed her into the kitchen.

'So, Sean tells me you're living with Zach at the moment.' Ally tugged open a cupboard and removed a bottle of gin. 'What can I get you to drink? Gin and tonic? Wine?'

'Just the tonic, please,' Keely said with a smile. 'I'm driving us home.'

'Home.' Ally gave a sigh and her expression was dreamy. 'That's so romantic. I never thought I'd ever see Zach involved with anyone.'

Oh, help!

'We're not involved,' Keely said hastily, glancing nervously towards the door and hoping that Zach wasn't within earshot. 'I've just moved in to help him out with his child-care crisis. Nothing more than that.'

'Oh.' For a brief moment Ally's face fell but then she smiled. 'All the same, living with each other—

well, one thing is bound to lead to another eventually, isn't it?'

'No!' Keely stared at her in consternation. 'It isn't like that—really.'

'Oh, come on, Keely.' Ally reached for a lemon and cut off several slices, which she popped into the glasses. 'You're the envy of the entire female population of Cumbria. Don't try telling me you don't find Zach attractive.'

'Don't you ever give up, Ally?' Zach's mild reproof came from the doorway and Keely blushed scarlet.

How much had he heard? Oh, no, he was going to think they'd been gossiping about him. She took a large slug of her drink, thoroughly embarrassed.

Ally, on the other hand, didn't seem at all embarrassed. She smiled broadly and handed Zach a drink.

'Just worrying about your welfare.' She slipped her arm through his and they walked towards the living room. 'So how's Phoebe been, Zach?'

'She's doing very well—which reminds me.' Zach's eyes flickered to Keely. 'She wanted you to go and give her a goodnight kiss.'

'No problem.' Relieved to have an excuse to get away from Ally's quizzical gaze, Keely hurried off to find Phoebe.

She took much longer than was necessary to settle the little girl down, curling up on the bed and reading her an extra story.

By the time she rejoined the rest of the adults, they were all seated at the table and Ally was placing an elaborate-looking starter in front of them all.

'It's a new recipe,' she declared with a flourish. 'You're guinea pigs.'

'Great. You really know how to whet someone's appetite.' Sean shook his head in exasperation as he looked at his pretty wife. 'You're not meant to tell the guests they're guinea pigs.'

'So how's general practice,' Zach asked Ally as he tucked into his starter. 'Still seeing all the usual trivia?'

'Trivia?' Ally glared at him and then subsided and smiled when she saw the twinkle in his eye. 'Zach Jordan, you're always winding me up and I fall for it every time. The answer to your question is that general practice is great and, no, I'm not seeing trivia.'

Keely took a sip of wine and looked at her shyly. 'Do you work full time?'

'Yes.' Ally glanced at Sean and laughed. 'But only three days a week in general practice. The rest of the time I'm a general slave and dogsbody.'

'Stop moaning, woman,' Sean growled, but his eyes twinkled and there was no missing the closeness between the couple.

Zach helped himself to a bread roll. 'Don't you ever miss real medicine?'

'No,' Ally said calmly, 'because I'm practising real medicine every day. It's you lot that work in a strange environment. Hospitals are totally alien places. You just treat symptoms there. Never people. In general practice we treat the whole person.'

Sean grinned. 'Since when did you need to treat the whole person to manage an ingrowing toenail?'

'Go ahead. Patronise me,' Ally said loftily, 'but I've lost count of the number of times we've had patients home from hospital—your hospital—with no end of problems that none of you managed to identify. The problem with hospitals is that each consultant just manages the bit he knows about. No one looks at the overall patient. That's what I do.'

Sean gave a smile. 'And you do it very well, angel. Your patients are damned lucky.'

Keely put her fork down, her appetite suddenly gone. Hearing Ally talk had made her realise just how much she didn't want to pursue a career in hospital medicine. She felt exactly the way that Ally did. That there was more to caring for a patient than managing a symptom.

Which wasn't going to make her much of a cardiologist...

'Are you all right, Keely?' Ally was looking at her, suddenly concerned. 'You look as though you've seen a ghost.'

'I'm fine.' Keely smiled at her through stiff lips. 'Tell me more about your job.'

'My job?' Ally shrugged and glanced round at the others. 'Well, why not? It's a quick way to irritate these two and that's always good for a laugh.'

She started to talk, telling them all about a patient who'd been admitted to hospital with a broken leg, about how they'd had to arrange for all her animals to be cared for.

'The hospital didn't even realise she had animals,' Ally said shortly, clearing the plates and standing up. 'Fortunately one of the neighbours saw the ambulance arrive to pick her up and came haring round here to ask us to sort it out. Which we did, of course.'

She took the plates into the kitchen and returned with the main course, a delicious chicken dish with rice.

'So what about you, Keely?' She served everyone and then looked at Keely curiously. 'Are you staying in A and E or are you doing a GP rotation?'

'Neither.' Keely picked up her fork and tried to summon up an appetite. 'I'm going to be a cardiologist.'

Except that she really, really didn't want to be one. Maybe she should talk to her father. Ask his advice. He was very career orientated but she knew that he loved her dearly. He wouldn't want her to do anything that she wasn't sure about.

'A cardiologist?' Ally glanced up and nodded. 'In Glyn Hughes's team?'

'Not Glyn Hughes's.' Zach's voice was strangely flat. 'Keely's not staying in Cumbria for long. She's going back to London at the end of her six months.'

Ally's face fell. 'You're not staying?' She looked visibly disappointed as she glanced from one to the other. 'But I thought—I assumed—'

'We all know what you assumed, sweetheart, but we'd rather you kept it to yourself,' Sean said gently, topping up her glass and giving her a smile. 'Now, buck up and eat your dinner before it gets cold.'

Ally ignored him, her eyes on Zach. 'I really hoped that—'

'Ally!' This time Sean's voice was sharp and Ally seemed to pull herself together.

'Sorry.' She turned her attention to her dinner. 'Cardiology. You must be a very clever girl, Keely.'

Keely shook her head, embarrassed by the sudden attention. She didn't feel clever. She felt confused. More confused than she'd ever felt in her whole life.

'We went sledding last week.' Zach picked up his wineglass and changed the subject neatly. 'The snow was fantastic.'

'Where did you go?' Sean topped up the rest of the glasses and they chatted about the snow for a while, swapping stories and anecdotes.

'I must admit it's the first time I've had a snowball thrown at me since I was about ten years old,' Zach said dryly, smiling across at Keely who stared at him, outraged.

'At least mine just hit you on the *outside*! You stuffed yours down my jacket! I nearly had frostbite.'

Ally glanced up, her face brightening. 'So, do you do lots of things together with Phoebe?' she asked casually, and Zach sighed.

'No, Ally. Generally we don't. The whole point of Keely living with me is that she's there to cover when I'm working so it's very rare that we're at home at the same time.'

Ally cleared her plate and put her knife and fork down thoughtfully. 'But Phoebe doesn't go to people very easily, does she, Zach? So she must really have taken to Keely.'

'She has taken to Keely,' Zach said, his smile exasperated. 'Now, drop it Ally. You're like a dog with a bone.'

'She's worse than that. She's embarrassing,' Sean

growled, glaring at his wife. 'I'd buy her a bow and arrow for Christmas so that she can play Cupid full time, but her aim is so lousy I dread to think what it would do for our workload in A and E.'

They all laughed and after that the evening improved and Keely found herself relaxing in their company.

By the time they scooped a sleeping Phoebe up from the bed and transferred her to the car, she was sorry to leave. The Nicholsons were a lovely family. And Ally was a lucky woman. Sean was drop-dead gorgeous and clearly very much in love with his pretty, if rather indiscreet wife.

'Thanks for coming.' Ally gave her a warm hug and then turned to Zach and lowered her voice. 'You should marry her, Zach. Snap her up quickly before she goes to London. She'd make a lovely mother for Phoebe.'

Keely sank into the driver's seat, mortified, relieved that she hadn't been able to hear Zach's reply. She could guess what it probably would have been.

He slid in next to her and she drove carefully out of the drive and into the tiny lane that led to the main road.

'I'm sorry about Ally.' Zach settled himself into his seat and closed his eyes. 'I did warn you that she was rather obsessed with pairing me up.'

'Yes.' Keely stared at the road, not daring to look at him. 'It doesn't matter.'

'Did she spoil the evening for you?'

She could feel his gaze on her and her hands tightened on the wheel. 'No. Not at all. I thought she was lovely.'

'She is, actually,' Zach agreed softly, 'just rather meddling.'

And very astute. Keely suspected that the other woman had had no trouble guessing exactly how she felt about Zach.

'Does she always try and pair you up with whoever you take there to dinner?'

'Well, I don't usually take women there to dinner,' he admitted with a wry smile, 'so I suppose in a way it was my fault. Taking you and admitting that you're living in my house is tantamount to putting an ad in *The Times* as far as Ally is concerned.'

'But she's tried matchmaking before?'

'On countless occasions.' He gave a short laugh. 'At one time or another I've been introduced to every one of Sean and Ally's single female friends.'

'How awful for you.' Keely's glance was sympathetic. 'Still, I suppose she means well.'

'She does indeed. And I suspect that her meddling streak makes her a very good GP.' He stifled a yawn. 'She knows everything there is to know about her patients and what makes them tick. What she does is very different to what we do, and whenever we get together we're always teasing each other.'

It certainly was different. And the more she thought about it, the more she thought it might be exactly what she wanted to do. Work in a small, country practice where she could get to know the patients inside out and help them. Not just deal with one crisis and then abandon them.

So what was she going to do?

There was no point in mentioning it to Zach. In fact, there was no way she *could* mention it to Zach. He'd assume that her change of heart was something to do with him. No. She'd have to do some research quietly by herself and then talk to her father.

CHAPTER EIGHT

THEY were working together the following morning when a young girl was brought in who'd collapsed.

Keely helped the ambulance crew move the patient onto the trolley and glanced at the girl's mother who was hovering anxiously in the doorway.

'What happened?'

'I really don't know.' The woman was obviously beside herself with panic. 'She was fine. Absolutely fine. One minute we were in a café together and the next minute she'd collapsed.'

Zach started to examine the girl. 'What were you eating?'

'Sorry?' The girl's mother looked at him blankly.

'What were you eating just before she collapsed?' Zach glanced at Keely. 'Let's get a line in, give her high dose oxygen and attach a cardiac monitor and a pulse oximeter. We need to get her stats above 94 per cent'

'Cake.' The mother looked confused. 'We were eating cake, but I don't see—'

'Is she allergic to anything that you're aware of?'

'Nuts.' The woman went pale. 'But there were no nuts in the cake. I checked.'

'Are you sure?' Zach turned to Nicky. 'She's wheezing badly. I want .3 mils of one in one thousand adrenaline. Give it intramuscularly, please.'

Nicky turned away to the drug trolley and Zach glanced at the mother. 'This is a very severe reaction. I think for the moment we'll have to assume that it was nuts.'

Nicky thrust an ampoule under Zach's nose and he read the label and nodded.

'Fine. And let's give her a 200 mg hydrocortisone IV and nebulised salbutamol.'

They worked for half an hour and finally the young girl was stabilised.

'Right.' Zach wiped his forehead with the back of his hand and gave the mother a tired smile. 'I'm going to refer her to the medical team. She needs to be admitted and we need to find out exactly what caused this reaction.'

The girl's mother nodded, obviously still worried.

'Will she be all right?'

Zach glanced at the girl and nodded. 'I think so. She seems stable now but I'm going to play it safe and admit her. It was a nasty reaction.'

They transferred the girl to the medical ward and Zach slumped against the wall, wearily surveying the mess in the room.

'I've got a really, really bad feeling about this week,' he muttered, and Nicky groaned as she tossed a discarded IV bag into the bin.

'Don't say that. Last time you had one of your feelings we were deluged with awful accidents.'

'I know that.' Zach straightened and rubbed a hand over the back of his neck. 'But look at the weather. The roads are like glass and people still insist on driving everywhere.'

No sooner had he said the words than the doors from the ambulance bay flew open and another accident victim was admitted.

After that there was a steady stream of patients and by the time Keely arrived home she was exhausted. So was Zach.

'That,' he said quietly, sinking into a chair in the kitchen, 'was a very bad day. Let's hope the rest of the week is better.'

It wasn't.

In fact, it got worse.

Every time the doors to A and E opened, drama followed, and by the end of the week Keely felt emotionally drained.

Dealing with critically injured patients was bad enough, but for Keely the worst bit was telling the relatives. Telling someone that their loved one had just died was the hardest thing she'd ever had to do.

'How do you do it?' she asked Zach one afternoon after they'd failed to resuscitate a twenty-year-old motorcyclist. 'How do you cope with telling them that their child is dead?'

Zach poured them both a cup of coffee, his face drawn. 'How do I cope? I suppose I switch off. I treat it as a job to be done. But it doesn't mean I don't feel it.'

He did feel it, Keely knew that. She'd seen the strain on his face after a week of repeated tragedy.

'I almost wanted to lie to those parents,' she admitted quietly, staring down at the coffee he handed her. 'The way they looked at me when I walked into the room, I wanted to tell them that there might be hope.'

'I know the feeling,' Zach said gruffly. 'But you mustn't ever do that. As it is, people find it hard to take in bad news. Harsh though it sounds, the only way to do it is to be blunt early on. And don't use euphemisms. Relatives will try very hard to misunderstand you because they don't want to hear the truth. If the patient is dead then you need to use the word ''dead'' very early on in the conversation and then use it several times. It's kinder in the long run.'

Keely looked at her coffee without enthusiasm. She didn't think her stomach would tolerate anything at the moment.

'Well, I'm seriously hoping not to have to use the word ''dead'' for a long time,' she said gloomily. 'I've used it enough this week to last me a lifetime. Surely we can't have any more tragedy.'

They did.

It was later in the afternoon when the hotline—the phone that connected straight to Ambulance Control—rang.

Nicky picked it up, listened and made notes, asked a few questions and then replaced the receiver.

'They're bringing in a four-year-old with difficulty breathing,' she told Keely quickly. 'I'll check everything in Resus. Will you make sure you're ready when they arrive?'

The doors to the ambulance bay crashed open only minutes later and the crew hurried in with mother and child.

Keely took one look at the child and turned to Nicky.

'I want the paediatric consultant, the Ear, Nose and Throat guys and an anaesthetist down here now!'

Quickly they took them into Resus and Keely pushed forward a chair.

'Sit down, Mrs Potter. Keep her on your lap.' She glanced at Nicky. 'Let's keep her with her mother so we don't upset her further, and give her some humidified oxygen, please.'

Zoe, the paediatric staff nurse, reached for the oxygen and placed a mask near the child's face, murmuring soothing noises as she did so.

The child looked severely ill, her face pale as she leaned forward on her mother's knee, drooling slightly.

'I need some details from you, Mrs Potter,' Keely said quietly, her eyes never leaving the child as she watched for any change in her condition. 'How long has she been ill?'

'Alice was fine yesterday.' The mother stroked the child's hair. 'I can't believe that she can have got like this so quickly.'

'Has she complained of any pain? Has she been coughing?'

'She said her throat was sore and she stopped eating because she couldn't swallow,' Mrs Potter said, and Keely nodded, her eyes still on little Alice.

The child was ominously quiet and Keely had a very, very bad feeling about her.

'Zoe, let's give her some nebulised adrenaline.' Hopefully that would buy her some time until the team arrived. She turned back to the mother. 'And has she had all her childhood immunisations?'

Mrs Potter suddenly looked wary. 'No. No, she hasn't. I don't believe in all that, I'm afraid. I think children are better off picking up the germs and developing their own immunity.'

Keely swallowed her frustration, reminding herself that everyone had the right to make their own choice about immunisation. The trouble was, she had a strong suspicion that Alice Potter was suffering from a disease that had been virtually eradicated thanks to the success of the vaccination programme.

'Shall I check her BP?' Nicky asked quietly, and Keely shook her head vigorously.

'No. Don't disturb her at all.'

Mrs Potter looked up. 'What's wrong with her?'

Keely took a deep breath. 'I think she has something called epiglottitis,' she said finally, and Mrs Potter frowned.

'I've never even heard of it.'

'It's extremely rare now,' Keely told her quietly, 'because most children are vaccinated when they're babies.'

Mrs Potter went slightly pale. 'But she'll be all right, won't she?'

Keely hesitated. 'She's seriously ill, Mrs Potter— very seriously ill.'

'Are you sure it's not just a bad sore throat?' Mrs Potter became slightly belligerent. 'You haven't even looked in her throat.'

'It could be very dangerous to look in her throat,'

Keely explained. 'If she is suffering from epiglottitis, examining her could totally obstruct her airway.'

Even as she watched, the child started to gasp for air and Keely turned to Nicky, her expression urgent.

'Let's get her on the trolley and call Zach quickly. And crash-bleep the paediatrician again. If he doesn't arrive soon I'll have to intubate her, and I'd like Zach here.'

'She's not breathing,' Zoe said quickly and Keely moved to the head of the trolley.

'OK, give me a small endotracheal tube and an introducer.'

While Zoe hurried the mother out of the room, Keely tried to intubate the child.

'It's all too swollen,' she muttered grimly as she tried to insert the tube into the little girl's airway. 'Damn. This is impossible. Give me an IV cannula—where the hell's Zach?'

'I'm right here,' came the calm reply, and she looked up with a sigh of relief.

'She's in respiratory arrest but I can't intubate her because her airway is so swollen. I'm going to do a needle cricothyroidotomy.'

With Zach's reassuring presence by her side she managed to perform the procedure successfully, and his quiet words of praise increased her confidence dramatically.

Then all of a sudden the room was full of people and the paediatricians took over.

'She's arrested.' Tony Maxwell snapped out some instructions and they all worked to save the little girl.

An hour later Tony shook his head, his expression

grim. 'I think we should stop now. Does everyone agree?'

'No!' Keely's cry was anguished. 'We've got to keep trying. She's only four years old.'

Zach put a hand on her shoulder and his voice was gruff. 'Keely, she's not responding.'

'But we can't let her die.'

'She's already dead,' Tony said gently, his eyes bleak as he looked down at the tiny figure on the trolley. 'Agonising though it is, I think we have to leave it at that.'

'It needn't have happened.' Keely felt a lump building in her throat and fought for control. Zach already thought she wasn't emotionally tough enough to cope with A and E work. She didn't want to prove him right. 'It's just so unfair...'

'I know.' Tony looked round and then his broad shoulders sagged slightly. 'OK, thanks, everyone.'

Keely took a deep breath. 'I'll tell the mother,' she said quietly, but Zach shook his head.

'Tony should do it, Keely. He's the senior paediatrician.'

Tony nodded, his expression glum. 'I get all the good jobs. Will you come with me, Nicky?'

The A and E nurse nodded and Keely noticed a tear shining in the corner of her eye.

So it wasn't just her, then...

'You did well, by the way.' Tony turned to Keely. 'I'm sorry we took so long to get here but we had an arrest in ITU.'

'I didn't manage to intubate her,' Keely mumbled, swamped by feelings of inadequacy. Surely there was something more she could have done? It all seemed so needlessly tragic. 'Maybe if I'd managed we'd have saved her.'

Tony shook his head. 'No one would have been able to intubate her,' he assured her calmly. 'Her airway was almost entirely obstructed. You did brilliantly. Better than most. And your diagnosis was spot on. Don't doubt yourself, Keely. You're a good doctor. A very good doctor.'

So why did she feel like such a failure?

Aware of Zach's scrutiny, Keely mumbled an excuse and walked out of Resus. At least her shift was over. Which meant she could go home and make a fool of herself in peace and quiet.

'Da-addy-y...' Phoebe hurtled out of the playroom and attached herself bodily to Zach's legs as he let himself into the house.

'Hello, trouble.' He stooped to pick her up, smiling at Barbara who'd followed her charge into the hallway. 'Has she been good?'

'Mostly.' Barbara had a twinkle in her eye that made Zach groan.

'Come on. What's she done?'

'She fed her toast into the video,' Barbara said calmly, 'but fortunately she sucked the butter off it first, so there was no long-term damage.'

'And?' There was more. He could tell. Zach braced himself.

'And...' Barbara glanced down at the sheepish toddler and gave her a wink. 'We actually had a small accident with a pen and the sitting-room wall, but it's all sorted out now.'

Zach closed his eyes and muttered something under his breath. 'Anything else I need to know?'

'She managed to dial 999 on the telephone.'

Zach winced. 'Who do I have to call to apologise?'

'I've done it.' Barbara bent down and picked the little girl up. 'The only thing I haven't solved is the problem of last week's copy of the *Lancet*. It was by your bed…'

Zach's eyes narrowed. 'And dare I ask where it is now?'

'In the bath,' Barbara told him cheerfully. 'Or, to be exact, drying on the radiator, having had a wash in the bath. My fault entirely. I turned my back to get a towel.'

Zach groaned. If he lost Barbara he didn't know what he'd do. 'What can I say?'

'Absolutely nothing,' she said firmly. 'I love her to bits. She's very bright and busy. Just as a healthy toddler should be.'

Zach shook his head in disbelief and kissed his daughter's face.

'You're a handful, madam.'

'More kiss.' Phoebe leaned towards him and he grinned and kissed her again, glancing up the stairs as he did so.

'Is Keely home?'

'Yes.' Barbara's smile faded and she gave a worried frown. 'To be honest, I thought she looked a bit upset. She's in the bathroom and she's been in there for ages.'

Zach's mouth tightened. And he could guess what she was doing. Crying her eyes out.

'Don't worry.' He scooped his daughter up and gave the older woman a smile. 'I'll go and see her.'

'Good. I'll be off then.'

Zach loosened his tie and took the stairs two at a time, Phoebe's arms clutched tightly round his neck.

'Keely?' He called her name through the bathroom door but there was no answer and he cursed under his breath.

'Keely!'

He thumped a fist on the door and Phoebe's bottom lip trembled and her arms tightened around his neck.

'Daddy no shout. Daddy noisy. Daddy say sorry.'

Before he could answer he heard Keely's voice, slightly muffled from the bathroom.

'I'm OK, Zach. I'm just having a bath.'

He didn't believe her for a moment, but he was helpless to do much with Phoebe in his arms. He'd put her to bed first and then sort out Keely.

It was half an hour before he returned to the locked bathroom door, and there was still no sign of Keely.

He called her again and finally she opened the door.

She was wrapped in a towel, the ends of her blonde hair damp from the steam and her sweet face blotched with tears.

'Zach!' She scowled at him and tried to brush away the traces of tears, obviously annoyed that he'd caught her crying. 'I just wanted to be alone.'

'I was worried about you.'

'Well, I'm OK.' Conscious of her nakedness beneath the towel, a soft blush touched her cheeks. 'Leave me alone, Zach.'

'No.'

'Why not?'

'Because you're upset,' he said calmly, lifting a hand to brush a blonde strand of hair away from her face. 'And I think you'd feel better if you talked about it.'

She glared at him. 'You never talk about your feelings—why should I?'

She looked so sweet and defensive he could barely keep his hands off her.

Her half-naked body was testing his self-control to the limits, and the sooner he got her dressed the safer it would be for both of them.

'Why don't you come out of the bathroom,' he suggested, 'and we can talk about it downstairs?'

'I don't want to talk about it,' she mumbled. 'I just want to be left in peace.'

'Well, that's one thing I'm not going to do.' He lifted one dark eyebrow in her direction. 'Are you coming out or am I carrying you out?'

The tears welled in her huge eyes and her voice shook. 'She was only four years old, and if her mother had had her immunised it never would have happened…'

Damn.

Zach reached for her, quickly wrapping her in his arms.

Keely started to sob into his chest, great tearing

sobs that shook her whole body and made him feel totally helpless.

'Hush, sweetheart…' He held her tightly and whispered nonsense into her hair until finally she was too exhausted to sob any longer. Then he lifted her into his arms and sat down on the bathroom chair with her on his lap.

'It's so unfair.' Her words were jerky. 'She didn't have to die. How will that poor mother cope with losing her child?'

'I don't know.'

Zach felt as sad about it as she did. In fact, he almost envied her ability to let her emotions out. Sometimes he wished he could do the same.

'Tell me honestly, Zach.' She wiped her eyes on the back of her hand. 'Was there anything else I could have done? What if I'd given her antibiotics straight away?'

He shook his head and stroked her hair away from her damp cheeks with a gentle hand. 'You did everything absolutely right. It was textbook management of a case of epiglottitis. We were all incredibly impressed that you even recognised it, to be honest. It's very rare these days.'

'But not rare enough,' she said in a quiet voice, leaning her face against his broad chest.

Zach tried not to react, reminding himself that she was just using him for comfort. But unfortunately his body wasn't that discerning and his immediate response to the soft scent of her hair and the warmth of her body made him grit his teeth.

'Let's get you dressed,' he said gruffly, hoping that

she'd move before he embarrassed himself, 'or you'll catch cold.'

'No, don't let me go. Not yet.' She snuggled closer and he stifled a groan.

Any minute now she'd realise the effect she was having on him.

'Keely…'

She lifted her head to look at him and her tear-washed eyes and trembling mouth were only inches away from his. And the temptation was just too much…

With a groan he lowered his head and captured her mouth, and the tension that had been building for weeks exploded between them.

Slowly at first, his lips moved over hers, the tip of his tongue seeking entry between her softly parted lips as he savoured the taste of her.

He felt her tremble in his arms and then her tongue touched his as she returned the kiss, her immediate and passionate response to his touch sending desire roaring through him like a runaway train.

Without breaking the kiss, his fingers tugged at the towel, leaving her naked in his lap.

'Zach…' She gasped his name against his mouth and then her tongue licked at his lips again, tantalising and teasing him until he was ready to forget the preliminaries and make love to her on the floor of the bathroom.

But she deserved better than that…

Battling with his instincts, he slipped his arms around her and stood up, intending to take her to the bedroom, but she gave a murmur of protest and tightened her arms round his neck.

'No, Zach.' Her voice was almost a sob. 'Don't let me go.'

Dear God, she was enough to test the will-power of a saint. Zach's fingers tightened into her warm satiny flesh. *He had no intention of letting her go...*

Their mouths fused again and they kissed desperately, biting at each other, trying to get closer—and closer still...

'The bedroom, Keely.' He murmured the words against her mouth but she gave a moan of protest and wriggled out of his arms, sliding down his body until she was on her knees, her fingers shaking as they dealt with his zip.

And then he felt her soft mouth touch him, her tongue and lips tasting and teasing him until he thought he'd explode.

'Keely...' His fractured groan of disbelief brought no response from her as she continued with intimacies that left him stunned and shell-shocked.

Finally, when he could stand it no longer, he lifted her roughly to her feet and backed her against the wall, his mouth devouring hers with a wild hunger that took them both past the point of no return.

In a smooth movement he lifted her and she wrapped her legs around his hips, her breath coming in pants as she felt his hardness brush against her.

'Please, Zach, please...'

She was sobbing with need and her soft gasps and the incredible liquid warmth of her body left him totally unable to control his actions.

His mouth still holding hers, he angled her hips and surged into her, taking her hard and fast, surrendering to the mindless passion that overwhelmed both of them.

He felt her body tighten around his and then she cried out his name, quivering and shaking in his arms, her frantic movements driving him over the edge into ecstasy.

For endless seconds they clung together, breathing heavily, and then he lowered her gently to the floor, his hands supporting her as her knees buckled.

Stunned by the power of the emotions that had erupted between them, Zach struggled to control his breathing and then bent his head to look at the shiny mass of blonde hair that was buried in his chest.

She was unbelievable. So sweet. *And so incredibly sexy…*

He slipped a gentle hand under Keely's chin and lifted her face, urging her to look at him.

Her cheeks were flushed and there was just a hint of shyness in her eyes, as if she didn't quite know what to say to him. Which was understandable, because he didn't know what to say to her either.

There had been a lack of control about their lovemaking—a primitive edge that had left them both shaken.

Her beautiful blue eyes looked nervous and her voice was no more than a whisper. 'Whatever you're about to say, Zach, please, don't tell me that you regret what we just did…'

The idea was so ridiculous that he almost laughed.

How could she possibly think he could regret an experience like that?

'The only thing I regret is not taking more time over it,' he said softly, stroking her tousled blonde hair away from her flushed cheeks with a gentle hand. 'You deserve more than a quickie in my bathroom. Did I hurt you?'

'No. It—it was fantastic.' Her softly whispered words and the deepening flush on her cheeks made his guts clench.

With a slow smile he scooped her up in his arms and bent his head to kiss her gently on the mouth.

'It certainly was. So fantastic we're going to do it again. Only this time we're not rushing it.' He opened the bathroom door and shouldered his way through to the landing. 'This time we're going to take all night.'

Keely lay in the bed, her eyes closed, a deliciously warm feeling spreading over her body.

Zach was an insatiable lover…

After their one, breathtakingly powerful encounter in the bathroom he'd proceeded to make love to her for the entire night in almost every position imaginable.

She blushed slightly when she remembered some of the things she'd allowed him to do to her—things she'd been much too shy to allow anyone else to do before. But, somehow, with Zach everything felt right.

And Fiona had been right on that first day when she'd guessed that Zach would be good in bed. He was better than good. He was incredible. He knew exactly where to touch her—how to touch her—to drive her totally wild with excitement. And his body...

Talking of his body, where was he?

She glanced around the room and decided that he must have gone downstairs. Had she slept that late?

She reached out an arm to grab the clock and gasped. Oh, help. They were both supposed to be working that morning and if she didn't get a move on she'd be late.

Keely showered in record time, pulled on her clothes and made her way down to the kitchen.

Suddenly she felt impossibly shy. What should she say to Zach? How should she react? It was pretty hard to pretend to behave normally after everything they'd shared the night before.

She paused in the doorway and then took a deep breath and walked into the kitchen, her cheeks slightly pink as she glanced at him.

'You should have woken me up.'

'You were totally out for the count.'

His voice was noticeably cool and Keely felt as though she'd been showered with cold water.

Why wasn't he looking at her?

Phoebe was in her high chair, fighting with a plate of food in her usual manner, and Keely sat down next to her.

'Your father rang.' Zach handed her a cup of tea and she stared at him blankly.

Her father?

Why would her father ring?

'D-did he leave a message?'

'Yes.' Zach's tone was even. 'You've got an interview in London in a few weeks. Congratulations.'

Keely looked at him in silence.

Was that all he was going to say? After everything they'd shared—everything they'd done? All he could say was, 'Congratulations'?

'Don't forget to ask Sean for the day off.' He was so matter-of-fact that she wondered whether she'd imagined everything that had happened between them the night before.

Had the whole thing been a dream?

Why wasn't he trying to stop her? Why wasn't he trying to talk her out of going?

Didn't he mind that she might move to London?

Obviously not, she thought dully, staring down at the piece of toast on her plate.

Last night had obviously been nothing more than a diversion for him. Something to briefly take his mind off his wife.

So that was that.

Last night she'd been so sure that he'd felt something for her. So sure.

But he was making it all too clear that he considered their night together to have been a mistake. He didn't want her and she certainly wasn't throwing herself at him again.

Which meant she may as well go to London.

She couldn't carry on living with Zach after last night. It would be too much to bear.

CHAPTER NINE

'YOU look awful.' Nicky opened the fridge to get some milk and frowned across at Keely who was sitting slumped in an armchair in the corner of the staffroom.

'Thanks for that.' Keely drained her coffee and stood up, knowing that it wouldn't take Nicky long to guess what was wrong.

And she didn't want to talk about it.

She *couldn't* talk about it.

Not without making a complete and utter fool of herself.

She walked briskly across to the door but Nicky's voice stopped her in her tracks.

'Keely, wait.' Nicky caught up with her and put a hand on her shoulder, her eyes searching. 'I suppose it's Zach?'

Was it that obvious?

Keely opened her mouth to deny it but then decided that she may as well be honest.

'Yes,' she mumbled. 'It's Zach.'

Nicky groaned. 'Oh, Keely, I warned you.'

'I know that,' Keely said, bravely dredging up a smile. 'I should have listened harder.'

'I'll kill Zach,' Nicky muttered, and Keely shook her head and ran a hand through her hair.

'It isn't his fault, Nicky,' she said wearily. 'It's

170

my fault. All my fault. He warned me that he'd never get involved with another woman and I wouldn't listen. I was so crazy about him I just wanted to help him. I thought I could do that without getting hurt myself. But then he—we—' She broke off and Nicky gave a groan.

'You don't have to tell me. I can guess.' There was a slight pause while Nicky digested what she'd just heard. 'And is it over? Are you sure?'

'Yes.' Keely nodded and managed a wan smile. 'You were right. He just won't ever get involved with another woman after his wife.'

Nicky frowned. 'Has he told you he's not interested?'

'Yes.' Keely paused. 'Well, not lately, I suppose. But after we actually... To be honest, he didn't say anything at all, but it didn't take a genius to work out that he wasn't interested.'

'Why? What did he do?'

Keely frowned and shook her head, still puzzled by it herself. 'He was so cold and distant. I couldn't believe it. We'd been so close, Nicky...' Her eyes filled and she cleared her throat. 'Damn. Sorry. When I woke up he was already downstairs and he was like a different person.'

'Right.' Nicky was looking at her thoughtfully. 'So something happened between him leaving your bed and you coming down for breakfast.'

'Nothing happened.' Keely gave a shrug. 'What could have happened? He got Phoebe up, gave her breakfast and took a phone call from my father. Nothing earth-shattering, I can assure you.'

'A phone call from your father?'

'Yes.' Keely rubbed her aching temples with her fingers. 'He rang to tell me I've got an interview in London in a few weeks.'

'And what did Zach say about that?'

Keely gave a humourless laugh, unable to hide the hurt. 'He said congratulations and reminded me to ask Sean for the time off.'

Nicky stared at her. 'That was it?'

'Yes,' Keely mumbled with a watery smile. 'He wasn't bothered, Nicky. In fact, he's probably pleased. It gets him out of having to tell me he'll never love me as much as his wife.'

'You don't know that.'

'Yes, I do.' Keely's voice was flat. 'Zach isn't interested in making a commitment to another woman. You know that as well as I do.'

Nicky let out a long breath. 'So what happens now?'

'I'm going to have to move out.' Keely made the decision on the spot. 'I can't carry on living there. Not now. It would be too difficult. I'm sure that Barbara will help with Phoebe until he can find someone else.'

Just thinking of little Phoebe made her heart twist. She'd got so used to the wonderful evening routine of bathing the little girl and giving her cuddles while she read a story. Giving that up would be almost as bad as giving up Zach.

Nicky gave her a quick hug. 'If it's any consolation, he's let you closer to Phoebe—and to him—than any other woman.'

'Well, it doesn't feel like a consolation at the moment,' Keely muttered, swallowing down an enormous lump in her throat.

Oh, for goodness' sake!

She was being totally pathetic. He'd been totally straight with her right from the beginning. She had no right to drip around, feeling sorry for herself.

Nicky shrugged helplessly, her expression sympathetic. 'Keely, I don't know what to say…'

'There's nothing you *can* say,' Keely said stoutly, glancing at her watch and deciding that the sooner she buried herself in work the better. 'Just hope I find somewhere to live fast. Before I make a fool of myself in front of him.'

'Well, that's easily solved. You can move in with me if you like,' Nicky said quickly. 'Our cottage isn't large but we've got a nice spare room which you're very welcome to.'

'That's really kind of you…' the lump in her throat grew bigger '…and if I get desperate I might take you up on it but, frankly, I think I'd be better off on my own.'

She felt so utterly miserable about Zach and Phoebe that she knew she'd be lousy company and she didn't want to have to keep putting on a brave face.

Nicky looked concerned. 'Are you sure you'll be all right staying with Zach until you find somewhere?'

'Oh, yes. We're on different shifts this week,' Keely said glumly. 'We overlap at work in the afternoons but we won't be seeing each other at home. I should survive.'

Or at least she hoped she would.

Thankfully they were incredibly busy over the next week, which helped Keely survive the trauma of seeing Zach every day and not being able to touch him.

It was still difficult.

She tried not to look at his familiar dark features, tried not to torture herself with memories of what they'd shared.

As for Zach, he seemed tired. Which didn't really make sense, she mused. To her knowledge he hadn't had any late nights and he hadn't been on call. So why did he have fine lines around his blue eyes and why was he so uncharacteristically impatient with people?

'Ouch,' said Nicky one morning after all of them had been on the receiving end of his biting sarcasm. 'I'm going for a cup of coffee to get out of the line of fire.'

'He's never normally like that,' Adam grumbled, looking quite white after the dressing-down he'd just received from the consultant. 'I don't know what's the matter with him.'

'I do,' Nicky said softly, glancing at Keely and giving her a knowing look. She waited until Adam left the room and then lowered her voice. 'I think you'll find that our handsome consultant isn't finding it as easy to give you up as he thought he might. Hang in there, kiddo, you might just find that this has a happy ending.'

But Keely knew there was no chance of that. If he wanted to have a relationship with her, why didn't he just say so? He must have guessed how she felt about him.

No. The only reasonable explanation was that he really didn't want to pursue anything between them.

At home they were like polite strangers—behaving as if their night of incredible passion had never happened.

If only she didn't have to see him every day, Keely thought glumly. It just reminded her of all the reasons why she'd fallen for him in the first place. He was such a brilliant doctor that watching him in action was enough to make anyone fall for him. And they did. She could hardly fail to notice that most of the nurses cast covert glances in his direction all the time—and some of the female doctors, too!

His skill and intuition as a doctor was brought home to her later that afternoon when a young woman was admitted having fainted in the shops.

'She just collapsed on me,' her husband said, the anxiety showing in his face. 'She's never fainted before to my knowledge. Never.'

'Right, well, let's get her on a trolley and examine her,' Keely said, frowning slightly as she looked at the woman. She was ashen and slightly sweaty and Keely didn't like the look of her at all.

'Nicky, let's get Zach in here, please,' she said in a calm voice and the A and E nurse left the room quickly, obviously picking up just how worried Keely was.

Zach was by her side in a matter of minutes, his handsome face serious as he questioned the husband.

The woman moaned softly, opened her eyes and then gave a little shriek and clutched her stomach.

'Oh, help me…'

'Is that where it hurts?' Instantly Zach's eyes flickered to the husband. 'Could I ask you to wait outside, please, while I examine your wife?'

The husband frowned and clutched his wife's hand. 'I'd rather stay.'

'I'll call you back in straight away,' Zach said gently, 'but I just need to take a look at her. I'm sure you understand.'

Nicky took the husband by the arm and led him out of Resus, and Zach immediately turned back to the woman.

'Does it hurt anywhere else?'

'My shoulder,' the woman gasped, and Keely stared at her, baffled. Zach's questioning was obviously aiming in a certain direction but at the moment she couldn't see what it was.

'Is there any possibility that you could be pregnant, Mrs Blythe?' Zach asked quietly, and the woman shook her head vigorously.

'No!' She gave a whimper and clutched her stomach again. 'Ow, it hurts!'

Zach was watching her closely. 'And when was your last period?'

'I don't know.' She avoided his eyes. 'I'm never regular.'

'Can you give me a rough date?'

Keely stepped forward and gave the frightened

woman a gentle smile. 'Don't be scared, Mrs Blythe. We have to ask these questions to find out what's wrong with you. Everything you say to us is confidential.'

The woman started to sob. 'I don't know what's wrong. I haven't had a period for eight weeks, but I can't be pregnant.'

'All right.' Zach's blue eyes narrowed slightly. 'I'm just going to examine your stomach, Mrs Blythe. Try and relax for me. What method of contraception do you use?'

'The coil,' she answered, and Keely watched while Zach examined her and then glanced at Nicky, his expression calm.

'Get me two large cannulae—12 or 14 gauge—get her cross-matched for six units of blood and request rhesus status. Nicky, I want a pregnancy test, please, and fast-bleep the gynaecology team.'

Keely listened to his list of instructions, her eyes fixed on his calm features. Despite his totally cool manner, he was obviously worried. Very worried. He was getting ready to resuscitate a potentially shocked patient—he obviously thought that Mrs Blythe was seriously ill.

Nicky and one of the staff nurses swung into action while Keely gave the woman some oxygen and prepared to take some bloods.

Suzy Blythe stared at them with frightened eyes. 'What's wrong with me?'

'You have a ruptured ectopic pregnancy,' Zach said gently, 'which basically means that the fertilised egg has implanted somewhere other than your uterus—usually one of the tubes that carry it to the uterus. That's what's causing the pain, and that's why you fainted.'

Keely stared at him.

How did he know that? There was no doubt or uncertainty in his voice at all. He was completely confident in his diagnosis.

'I can't be pregnant!'

Zach's gaze rested on the young woman's frightened face. 'Why?'

'Because my husband's been away for the last six months,' she sobbed, her whole body trembling. 'I can't be pregnant. I just can't be.'

Keely held her breath. Was Zach wrong?

'Suzy…' Zach took a deep breath and his voice was incredibly patient. 'Believe me, we're not here to judge you. We just want to make you well. You have a very serious condition, which I'm sure is an ectopic pregnancy.'

Suzy's cried harder. 'I don't know what to do.'

Zach's voice was gentle. 'But you could be pregnant?'

There was a long silence, broken only by Suzy's sobs. 'Yes. It was just the once,' she admitted jerkily, her tear-stained face contorting as another pain hit her. 'Oh, heavens, what am I going to do? What will Rob say?'

'Don't worry about that now.' Keely gave her shoulder a squeeze, feeling desperately sorry for her.

Zach quickly finished his physical examination. 'Have you had any vaginal bleeding, Suzy?'

'No. Nothing.'

'The pregnancy test is positive, Mr Jordan,' the staff nurse said quietly, her eyes fixed adoringly on Zach's face.

Keely gritted her teeth and felt a powerful surge of jealousy, which shocked her. Why should she be jealous? She had no right to be jealous. He wasn't hers. And she could hardly blame the nurse for drooling over him. If she found the man irresistible, why shouldn't everyone else?

'Keely, take bloods for FBC, U and Es, blood sugar and G and S,' Zach ordered, 'and call the gynae team and tell them she's going to need to go to Theatre.'

'Will they tell Rob?' the woman whispered, and Zach gave a sigh.

'I'll have a word with the consultant who'll do the operation. The answer is, I don't know. It depends on what happens in Theatre.'

Keely helped prepare the woman for transfer to Theatre for a laparoscopy—an operation which would allow the surgeons to look inside her abdomen.

When she returned, Zach was making himself a cup of coffee in the staffroom.

Bother. She'd been hoping to have five minutes by herself. But, still, she could use it as an opportunity to pick Zach's brains. She was still stunned and impressed that he'd known instinctively what the matter was with the woman.

'How did you know it was an ectopic pregnancy?' Maybe if she kept it professional they'd be able to have a conversation without her wanting to throw herself into his arms.

'I've seen it before,' Zach told her, adding milk to his coffee and stirring it slowly. 'Several times, in fact. She was lucky. She had a stable form. In the unstable form it's often touch and go.'

Keely still didn't understand how he'd reached his diagnosis so quickly. 'But it could have been any number of other things.' She ticked them off on her fingers. 'Appendicitis, a gastrointestinal bleed—'

'True. But the first thing you exclude in a woman of childbearing age suffering from abdominal pain is ectopic pregnancy,' Zach told her, taking a sip of coffee and dropping into one of the armchairs. 'It's important to assess risk factors to see how likely it is.'

Keely was confused. 'But she told you she couldn't be pregnant so it didn't seem likely. Why didn't you believe her? I think I would have just taken her at her word, and then what would have happened? How did you *know*, Zach?'

'How did I know?' He gave a sigh and stretched long muscular legs out in front of him. 'Firstly, because she was of childbearing age and her symptoms suggested it. Secondly, because her body language suggested that she wasn't telling the truth—'

'But how did you know that?'

She would have missed it, she knew she would.

He shrugged. 'Experience.'

Keely's shoulders sagged. 'But I wouldn't have pushed her like you did. I don't think I would have had the nerve to do a pregnancy test when she'd told me that she couldn't be pregnant.'

'On the contrary, you handled it very well,' Zach said quietly. 'You spotted instantly that her condition could be serious and you called a senior doctor, which was absolutely the right decision. You were kind and approachable and I suspect that if I hadn't forced her to tell me, she would have eventually confided in you.'

'But you knew what was wrong with her,' Keely said gloomily, 'and I didn't have a clue. I haven't got your instincts.'

'You haven't got my experience,' he corrected her gently. 'There's nothing wrong with your instincts. Your instincts are fine. Stop beating yourself up.'

Their eyes locked and awareness sizzled between them.

With a muttered curse Zach thumped his mug down on the table and stood up abruptly. His broad shoulders tensed and his blue eyes were suddenly wary. 'Keely, we need to talk.'

'Yes.' Her voice was little more than a whisper. 'I suppose we do.'

'At home. It's more private.'

'I thought you were working late tonight?'

'Sean swapped with me,' he said smoothly, 'so that I can be home in time to put Phoebe to bed.'

'But I could have done that,' she protested as he walked over to the sink and put his mug on the draining-board.

'Thanks.' He kept his back to her. 'But I'd rather

do it myself. It's one of the things I need to talk to you about.'

In other words, he didn't want her near his daughter.

Keely watched him go and felt more miserable than she ever had in her life. If he was going to those lengths to keep her away from his daughter then it was definitely time that she moved out.

Zach was in the kitchen when she arrived home, and he got straight to the point.

'I'm sorry, but this isn't working out any more, Keely.' His eyes were steady on hers. 'You'll be off to London in no time at all. It's time Phoebe got used to not having you around.'

'You want me to move out?'

She'd planned to do just that, so why did it feel so painful when he suggested it?

'She's getting too attached to you.' He ran a hand through his sleek, dark hair, obviously finding the conversation difficult. 'I don't want to see her hurt.'

'Neither do I, Zach.' Did he really think she wanted to hurt his daughter?

'I know you don't, but nevertheless that's what's going to happen when you leave. And it's just going to get harder the longer you stay.'

'Yes. I see that.' Her voice sounded strangely flat. Totally unlike her own. 'I'll start looking for somewhere else to live.'

He rubbed his fingers over his clenched jaw, visibly tense.

'Listen, Keely…' He hesitated, obviously struggling to find the right words. 'We haven't talked about what happened between us but—'

'No.' She held up a hand and interrupted him before he could say any more. 'Don't say it. There isn't anything that needs to be said.'

It was true. What could he say that wouldn't make her feel a million times worse?

She didn't need him to spell out the way he felt.

He looked at her warily. 'I'm really grateful for your help with Phoebe.'

Keely ignored the hurt and gave him a brave smile. 'You're very welcome, Zach. I hope it works out for you both. I'll start looking for somewhere else to live tomorrow. Can I stay here until I find somewhere?'

He frowned. 'Of course, but—'

'Thanks.' She stroked her blonde hair behind her ears and walked towards the door, anxious to put as much distance between them as possible. 'Well, I've got to prepare for my interview so if you'll excuse me I'll go upstairs.'

With that she turned on her heel and took refuge in the sanctuary of her bedroom.

The next two days were frantic and Keely barely had time to breathe, let alone make phone calls about flats.

She arrived at Zach's house at the end of the second day in time for Phoebe's bath and wondered what she was meant to do.

Zach had made it clear that he didn't want her near Phoebe so she'd been avoiding the little girl as much as possible, but if Barbara needed to leave to get home to her own family then surely Zach wouldn't mind if she helped out?

She opened the front door and stopped dead as she saw a stunning blonde woman standing in the hallway.

'Hello?' Keely frowned in confusion and closed the front door behind her. 'I don't think we've met…'

'No.' The woman held out her hand and gave a formal smile. 'I'm Maggie Hillyard. The new nanny.'

The new nanny?

Zach had employed a new nanny?

The man certainly didn't hang around.

'Are you…?' Keely cleared her throat and started again. 'Will you be living in?'

'Oh, yes.' Maggie nodded. 'Zach was quite insistent. He's given me the room at the back until you move out. When you've gone I'll have your room because the view's better. I gather you're looking for somewhere at the moment.'

Keely's lips were so stiff she could barely form the words to reply. 'That's right. So when did you get the job?'

When exactly had Zach decided to employ a new nanny? And what had happened to dear Barbara?

'Mr Jordan interviewed me a few days ago,' the nanny said crisply. 'The poor man was obviously desperate for me to start as soon as possible. He told me that you had to leave in a hurry and that he was looking for a replacement.'

Keely tried not to mind that the description made her sound like an employee. She wasn't an employee.

She hadn't cared for Phoebe because it had been part of a job description. Or because she'd been paid. She'd cared for Phoebe because she loved her. With all her heart and soul.

'You're right.' She smiled at the other woman, although the smile felt so unnatural that she thought her skin might crack. 'I do have to leave.'

The hope—the little that she'd managed to hold onto—had drained out of her as the new nanny spoke, and she knew she *did* have to leave. She no longer had a choice. If Zach was prepared to go to these lengths to keep her away from his daughter then it was time she faced facts. And the facts were that Zach Jordan had been so badly hurt that nothing could heal the wounds inside him—no amount of love or devotion would solve his problems. He was never going to change his mind and ask her to stay.

'In fact, I was leaving tonight.' Her decision made, she gave the woman another false smile and took the stairs two at a time, walking briskly to her bedroom, careful not to look in on Phoebe who was asleep. She was going to miss the little girl as much as she'd miss Zach.

In her room, she grabbed her clothes out of the wardrobe and stuffed them untidily into a suitcase, biting back the sobs that threatened to choke her. Not now. She couldn't break down now. Zach could be home at any minute and she just couldn't face him. She really couldn't.

Once the suitcase was full she delved into her bag for her mobile phone and called Nicky to check that her offer of accommodation still stood. Then she walked quickly downstairs and wished the nanny every happiness in her new job.

How long would it take the new nanny to fall for Zach? She walked briskly to her car and unlocked it. How long before Zach had to let her go as he had all the other nannies?

Keely slammed the car door shut and turned the key in the ignition with shaking fingers. Damn the man! Damn the man for making her love him, and for having such a lovely daughter.

Hot tears started to burn her eyes and she angrily dashed them away and reversed the car out of the drive. She held the tears back and drove until she was safely out of sight of Zach's house before pulling over and sobbing until she thought her heart would break.

She awoke in Nicky's spare bedroom cuddled under a warm, snug duvet covered in tiny flowers.

Her head throbbed and her eyes felt gritty from crying and lack of sleep.

There was a tap on the door and she struggled into a sitting position as the door opened and Nicky popped her head round the door.

'Are you decent? I've made you a cup of tea. It's six o'clock. You need to get a move on if you're going to work.'

Was she going to work? Going to work meant meeting Zach…

'I don't think I can face him, Nicky,' she croaked, and the other girl sighed and walked into the room.

'Yes, you can,' she said firmly. 'You could have

a day in bed, but what good would that do? You'd just cry your eyes out all day and that won't make you feel any better.'

It would feel better than bumping into Zach every other minute.

'I'm going to make a fool of myself—'

'No.' Nicky's voice was quiet. 'It's not you that's the fool in all this, Keely. It's Zach. If he's letting a girl like you go then, believe me, he's the fool. You're the best thing that's ever happened to him and the best thing that's happened to Phoebe, but he's too pig-headed to see it.'

'He's just been very badly hurt,' Keely whispered, reaching for her tea and taking a mouthful. 'And there's nothing I can do about that. I don't think he'll ever get over his wife. And how can I begin to compete with someone who isn't even around any more?'

'Don't think about that now. Have a shower,' Nicky advised. 'A long, hot shower. Wash your face and put some make-up on.'

'Oh, no!' Keely clapped her hand over her mouth in dismay. 'My make-up! I forgot to clear my things out of his bathroom. I was in such a state when I saw the nanny that I just wanted to get out of there as soon as possible. How am I going to cover the blotches on my face?'

'With some of mine.' Nicky picked up the empty mug and walked towards the door. 'My make-up box is on the bathroom shelf. Help yourself to anything you fancy. And there's a new toothbrush in the cupboard above the bath.'

Keely gave her a grateful look. 'What can I say?'

'Say that you're going to go to work.' Nicky's chin lifted slightly. 'And say that you're going to tell Zach how you feel about him.'

'No way.' Keely shook her head. 'I'm not throwing myself at him again. It's time I learned to take no for an answer.'

By the time she arrived at work she was relatively confident that she'd successfully removed all traces of her distress. She certainly looked pale and tired but, then, so did half of the doctors who worked in A and E. It was a stressful environment.

For the first few hours of the day she only saw Zach from a distance and then, just when she was beginning to relax, she walked into him in the corridor. Literally.

'Careful.' His strong hands gripped her shoulders and steadied her, and she stepped back as if she'd been burned.

'I'm sorry.' Dear God, she needed to get away from him. Fast.

Without saying anything further, she turned on her heel but he was too quick for her, his long fingers biting into her arm and holding her still.

'Wait a minute.' His voice was quiet and he was frowning slightly. 'Maggie tells me that you moved out last night. I didn't think you'd found anywhere yet. You didn't mention that you were leaving. Where did you go, Keely?'

'It really doesn't matter.' She'd rather keep it to herself for now. 'I'm fine, Zach.'

'Keely...'

He looked tortured and suddenly she realised that

it didn't matter how *she* felt. She just wanted *him* to be all right. She didn't want to cause him more pain. The man had had enough of that to last him a lifetime. It wasn't his fault that he couldn't love her the way he'd loved his wife.

'Really, truly I'm fine.' On impulse she stood on tiptoe and gave him a kiss on the cheek. 'You take care of yourself and Phoebe. Now, I've got to dash.' She lifted her chin and gave him a bright smile. 'I promised to help Nicky.'

Without waiting for his reply, she turned on her heel, hurrying down the corridor and back into the department before he could stop her.

CHAPTER TEN

SOMEHOW Keely stumbled through the next two weeks, working on autopilot and keeping her emotions firmly in check. By a stroke of luck Sean scheduled her to work nights, so the only contact she had with Zach was the occasional glimpse of his broad shoulders in the distance.

And then suddenly she was back on days again and avoiding him became harder.

'Zach was looking for you earlier—did he find you?' Nicky caught Keely in the corridor as she walked towards the common room late one morning.

'No. Thank goodness.' Keely pulled a face. 'I really can't face any more conversations with him at the moment.'

'Well, in that case come up to the canteen with me for something revolting to eat,' Nicky joked, obviously trying to cheer her up. 'It's just about lunchtime and we're not usually this quiet so we should make the most of it while we can.'

Keely pulled a face. The mere thought of food made her stomach churn. She hadn't eaten properly for days and a seed of worry was starting to grow at the back of her mind.

'No, thanks.' She certainly wasn't going to voice her suspicion to Nicky. 'Sean's given me permission to take a long lunch-break and I'm going to Zach's to pick up the things I left in his bathroom. He's working late tonight so I know there's no chance of running into him. I want to get it over with. I need a clear head for my interview so the sooner I'm out of his life the better.'

'OK.' Nicky gave her a worried smile. 'Well, for goodness' sake, be careful on the roads. They're icy.'

Despite the warning, Keely wasn't careful.

She drove too fast, as if her sudden burst of speed might help her outrun her problems.

She was only yards from Zach's house when she saw the smoke.

'Oh, my God, no!'

She slammed on her brakes and left the car at a run, sprinting the last few yards to Zach's house, her problems forgotten.

Zach's house was on fire!

Flames licked out of the upper windows and smoke billowed in huge clouds into the cold blue sky. A crowd of people had gathered at the end of Zach's path and Keely elbowed her way through, her heart lifting with relief when she saw Barbara standing at the end of the garden.

'Barbara—thank goodness you're safe. Were you inside?'

Barbara shook her head, her face pale with shock and anxiety. 'No. The new nanny was in charge.'

The new nanny?

Keely looked round frantically. Where was she?

'Barbara, have you seen her? The nanny? And where's Phoebe?'

Her heart was pounding and she felt the panic rise and threaten to swamp her.

Where was Zach's daughter?

'They're over there, under the tree.'

Keely glanced across and saw the nanny in conversation with a woman from the village. There was no sign of Phoebe.

Scanning the front garden frantically, Keely tried to stay calm. The child was bound to be here somewhere...

'The fire brigade are on their way,' Barbara told her. 'With any luck they'll be able to save Zach's house.'

But Keely wasn't thinking about Zach's house. She was thinking of Zach's daughter.

Where was Phoebe?

Her heart in her mouth, she sprinted over to the nanny, stumbling on the hard, frozen earth. It was so cold that everyone's breath was clouding the wintry air. 'Where's Phoebe?'

The nanny looked startled. 'She's playing under that tree...'

She turned to point her out to Keely and her face blanched. 'Oh, no, she's gone...'

Keely looked round frantically, yelling at the others to find the child.

'She's always wandering off,' the nanny grumbled. 'She'll be here somewhere.'

'It was your job to watch her,' Keely snapped. 'She's not even three years old. They all wander off at that age.'

Fergus, the four-year-old son of the farmer who

was Zach's nearest neighbour, stuck his finger out and pointed to the house.

'Phoebe's in the house,' he said firmly, and cold fingers of panic squeezed Keely's heart as she dropped to her knees and looked him straight in the eye.

'Phoebe's gone into the house? Are you sure?' Her voice was hoarse, and Fergus nodded.

'She wanted her teddy. She lost her teddy.'

Oh, dear God, if Phoebe was looking for her teddy then she knew exactly where the child would be.

In the playroom—right at the back of the house.

'I'm sure she isn't in the house,' Maggie said nervously, but Keely shot her a look of pure disdain.

'She's gone back to the house. She must have. Don't you know *never* to take your eye off a toddler?' Worry made her uncharacteristically rude. 'What sort of a nanny are you?'

Without waiting for a reply, she turned to look at Zach's house, which was rapidly becoming an inferno. And little Phoebe was in there, looking for her teddy...

Briefly her eyes closed and then she thrust Fergus into the arms of his mother with curt instructions not to let him go. Without stopping to think about the sense or safety of what she was doing, she sped towards the house, ignoring the shouts from behind her.

In the distance she thought she heard sirens but she knew she had to act immediately. Even a few minutes might be too late to save Phoebe.

Trying to remember what she knew about fires,

she took a few big gulps of clean air before dropping to her hands and knees in the smoke-filled hallway. Thank goodness the flames hadn't yet spread to that part of the house.

Stay low, she reminded herself firmly. Smoke rises.

Disoriented by the smoke in the hall, she tried to remember the way to the playroom, feeling her way along the wall, turning into the lounge and crawling rapidly into the extension at the back of the house. All around her bits of furniture crackled as the fire took hold and the smoke was so thick it choked her. Forcing down her fear, she paused and peered through the smoky gloom.

'Phoebe!' Her voice sounded odd above the crackle of the flames and she looked round frantically, feeling as though her lungs were going to burst. Where was she? There was no sign of her. Maybe Fergus had been wrong and she was outside, playing a game of hide and seek…

Overwhelmed by fear for Phoebe, she started to panic, her ability to think dulled by the smothering smoke and the pain in her chest.

And then she saw her.

Lying on the floor in a little ball. Unconscious.

Unconscious or dead?

No. Please, not dead.

Forcing herself not to think about that possibility, Keely battled to keep her rising panic in check. This was no time for even the most basic first aid. The best thing she could do for Phoebe now was get her out. If she didn't get her out, she'd die for sure—in fact, both of them would die...

Choking and coughing, she wriggled up to the body of the child and grabbed a handful of her jumper, dragging her along the floor towards the door. But this time her journey was impeded by the extra weight and the ever-building volume of smoke. She cried out and sobbed as a piece of burning wood fell onto her hand and she collapsed face down on the floor ready to give up.

She was going to die. They were both going to die. And Zach would lose his precious daughter.

First his wife and then his daughter.

No!

The thought of what such a loss would do to the man gave a final boost to her will-power and she drove herself forward, teeth gritted, barely breathing as the smoke grew denser. It felt as though her lungs were on fire and she started to cough and choke as she crawled nearer to the door.

Oh, God, please, let Phoebe live.

She didn't even care if *she* died any more. Her lungs and her hand hurt so much that she was ready to give up and let the smoke get her, but she wanted the little girl to live so badly she pushed herself through the pain barrier.

Keep going, just keep going, she told herself, and then finally, through the flames that were starting to lick their way into the hall, she saw the front door. Nearly there. *So nearly there.* But she couldn't make it. Her lungs were burning and she no longer had enough oxygen to continue, but she pushed Phoebe

as hard as she could towards the door, dimly aware
of a fireman in breathing apparatus grabbing the child
and carrying her to safety.

And then her breath scorched in her lungs and the
world went black.

'Burns coming in, Zach,' Nicky said briskly, hanging
up the hotline phone and scurrying towards Resus.

'Adult and child.'

Zach nodded, his eyes gritty from lack of sleep.
Phoebe had been up all the previous night, fractious
and unsettled because of the new nanny. She was
missing Keely's gentle warmth and, if he was honest,
so was he. He forced the thought aside and tried to
concentrate on the job in hand. 'Any details?'

'None.'

The hotline rang again and Nicky frowned. 'Not
another one. Don't do this to me,' she muttered, picking the phone up and tucking it under her ear.
'Hello?'

Zach watched idly, waiting to hear whether yet
another incident was about to descend on them.

'Oh, Lord, are you sure? Read me the address.'
Nicky's voice was little more than a whisper and her
face visibly paled as she swivelled to look at him.

And he knew.

Just by looking at the expression in her eyes, he
knew without a shadow of a doubt that the fire was
in his house.

Which meant that the child was—

'Phoebe!'

The ambulance siren shrieked outside the department and Zach was in the ambulance bay and dragging open the doors before they'd turned the engine off.

'Calm down, Zach.' Pete, one of the paramedics, gave his shoulder a quick squeeze. 'She seems OK. Maybe some minor smoke inhalation, but her resps have been fine and she's got no obvious burns.'

'Thank God.'

'It isn't God you should be thanking,' Pete said roughly. 'It's Keely. She ran into your house after the child and saved her life. If it hadn't been for Keely, Phoebe would definitely be dead, Zach. The girl's a bloody heroine.'

Keely?

Zach felt shell-shocked, his gaze shifting from the still form of his daughter to the other body on the stretcher in the ambulance. He hadn't even see that there was another person in the ambulance, he'd been so worried about his daughter.

'She had signs of laryngeal oedema so we've intubated her,' Pete told him. 'And she had morphine at the scene.'

Keely or Phoebe?

For a moment he couldn't take in what was being said. He couldn't think straight and he felt an unfamiliar panic grip him. Dragging a deep breath into his lungs, he forced himself to ignore the fact that it was Keely lying there, and that his precious daughter was injured, too. They needed his skills and he couldn't be objective unless he could switch off.

'OK.' He cleared his throat and pulled himself together, his expression grim. 'Let's get both of them into Resus.'

He scrambled out of the ambulance and sprinted back into the department. 'Nicky—get Tony Maxwell down here now and fast-bleep the first-on anaesthetist.'

He needed someone he trusted to look after his daughter while he concentrated on Keely. No way was he going to let her die. No way.

'Get her connected to an ECG monitor now—if she's inhaled smoke she might have arrhythmias, and let's measure carboxyhaemoglobin.' His instructions were terse. 'And get a line in, Adam. Move!'

Adam worked quickly and Sean Nicholson strode over to the trolley, his expression serious.

'I just heard. What do you want me to do?'

'Check on my daughter,' Zach said through gritted teeth. 'The paramedics told me they thought she was OK so I'm letting someone else deal with her.'

'I'll see to it,' Sean said quickly, moving across Resus to the other trolley.

'OK, Adam.' Zach looked up. 'Let's give her the highest possible concentration of humidified oxygen and get an IV up—we need to maintain circulating blood volume.'

'She's got a nasty burn on her hand,' Nicky said. 'Shall I dress it?'

'Let's get her stable first,' Zach said shortly. 'How are her vital signs?'

'She's doing well,' Adam said quickly. 'Her ECG is normal and her pulse and BP are stable.'

'Phoebe is going to be fine.' Sean appeared by

Zach's shoulder. 'No sign of smoke inhalation or burns. I suspect she breathed in and then fell to the ground and that probably saved her. Keely obviously got her out before any lasting damage was done.'

She'd saved his daughter.

Zach pushed the thought away. He couldn't think about that now. He was too busy saving her.

Sean moved closer. 'How's she doing?'

'All right, I think. I want to do a chest X-ray. We've sent off bloods and we need to sort out her hand.'

Sean took a quick look. 'It isn't too bad. Smother it in silver sulphadiazine cream, Nicky, and put it inside a sterile plastic bag.'

Nicky scurried to do as he'd instructed and Zach and Adam finished all the necessary investigations and management before transferring Keely to the ward.

Only once he was satisfied that Keely was stable did Zach return to comfort his daughter, and it was then that it hit him.

He'd nearly lost both of them...

Her chest hurt.

Keely opened her eyes and blinked several times, her vision blurred as she looked round the sterile hospital room.

'Zach...' Her voice barely functioned, little more than a hoarse croak coming from her lips as she tried to speak.

'I'm right here.' He was by her side in an instant and she felt a rush of panic.

'Phoebe?'

'Alive and well.' A muscle worked in his jaw. 'Thanks to you.'

'Oh, thank God…' She closed her eyes and swallowed hard. 'I really thought…'

She didn't want to tell him what she'd thought, but he read her mind and sat down on the edge of her bed, his hand covering her uninjured one.

'I can imagine what you thought. And I can't thank you enough, Keely.' He rubbed his forehead and shook his head slowly. 'I don't know what to say to you. I don't know how to even begin to thank you.'

'You don't have to thank me. I'm just glad she's all right. I was so worried.' Her voice was getting stronger and she didn't feel anywhere near as bad as she thought she should. 'My throat's sore, Zach.'

'It will be.' He nodded. 'You were intubated.'

Her eyes widened. 'Really?'

'Really.' He gave a tired smile. 'For a while back there it was touch and go. You gave me a fright.'

She closed her eyes and breathed out. 'You poor thing. You must have been so worried about little Phoebe.'

'I was equally worried about you,' he said quietly, his eyes fixed on her face. 'Whatever possessed you to take such a risk, Keely? To go into a burning house? You could have been killed.'

A vivid picture of the heat and the flames filled her mind and she shuddered.

'Don't talk about it—I've never been so scared in my life.'

His jaw tightened. 'But you still did it…'

'I had to find Phoebe.' Her face was serious.

'How did you know she was in there? Barbara said that no one had actually seen her enter the house. You could have been risking your life for nothing.'

'I knew she was in there.' Keely smiled weakly. 'She lost her bear again and she's always dropping it in the playroom. I didn't really have a choice. What if I hadn't gone in, Zach? By the time the fire engines arrived she'd have—'

'Don't!' He interrupted her roughly and shook his head, obviously unable to contemplate such an awful scenario. 'I just can't believe you took such a risk for my daughter.'

'I love her, Zach.'

His eyes locked with hers. 'I owe you so much.'

She shook her head and her eyes filled with tears. 'You don't owe me anything, Zach. I'm just glad she's OK. Where is she now?'

'On the ward. They're keeping her in for observation.'

'I'll pop down and see her later.' Keely looked hesitantly at Zach. 'That's if you don't mind, of course…'

Was he still anxious to keep her away from his daughter?

'Keely, don't!' Zach's voice was gruff and his grip on her hand tightened. 'Don't remind me what a total idiot I've been. Will you ever forgive me?'

He thought he'd been an idiot? What did that mean? What was he saying?

He looked at her steadily, his blue eyes searching every inch of her pale face.

'This really isn't the time or the place, but there's something I need to say to you.' His voice was rough and his grip on her hand tightened.

'Mr Jordan?' The ward nurse interrupted them, her expression serious. 'I'm sorry to disturb you but Paeds are on the phone. Your daughter is asking for you—and A and E have phoned twice while you've been up here. There's been a pile-up on the motorway and they're desperate for your help.'

Zach tipped his head back and muttered under his breath while Keely carefully hid her frustration. Obviously she was going to have to wait to find out what he wanted to say to her. The man was being pulled in different directions as usual.

The ward nurse looked apologetic. 'What shall I tell Paeds?'

Keely struggled into a sitting position. 'Tell them to bring Phoebe up here. I'll keep her company until her daddy has finished in A and E.' She glanced nervously at Zach. 'If that's OK with you, of course.'

What would he say?

Would he refuse?

Was he still trying to keep her away from his daughter?

'You're not well enough to entertain a toddler.' He frowned at her and she sank back onto her pillows.

'I'll be fine. I want to see her, Zach. The staff here will help—'

'Well, of course we will.' The nurse rose to the

challenge and gave Keely a wink. 'I've got a niece
and nephew of the same age so I'm sure I can cope
with your daughter on my ward.'

Zach and Keely exchanged smiles. The woman
had no idea of Phoebe's capacity for mischief.

'If you're sure you're up to it...' He leaned forward and brushed his lips against her forehead, a
look of frustration crossing his handsome features.
'There's so much I want to say to you but it's obviously going to have to wait. Tell Phoebe I'll be up
to see her when I've finished downstairs.'

She stared up at him, her eyes feasting on his firm
mouth and his dark jaw. His calm strength surrounded her and she felt deliciously warm and safe
after the horrors of the fire.

What did he want to say to her?

Keely watched him go and then closed her eyes,
forcing herself not to hope for something that wasn't
going to happen. In the meantime, she needed to talk
to the doctor. In private. There was something she
needed to ask him...

It was several hours later when Zach took the stairs
two at a time and pushed open the door to the ward.
He'd been in A and E longer than he'd planned and
he was worried about Keely.

'Oh, Mr Jordan.' The ward nurse intercepted him,
catching his arm and stopping him in mid-stride. 'I'm
going to have to ask you to be quiet, I'm afraid.
They're both asleep.'

'Asleep?' His brows met in a deep frown and he

glanced towards Keely's room. 'My daughter's asleep, too? Did you put another bed in the room?'

The ward nurse sighed and gave a rueful smile. 'I'm afraid not. It's against all the rules, of course, but your daughter was fretting so we overlooked it on this occasion. She's asleep in Dr Thompson's bed.'

Zach walked quietly to the side ward and paused in the doorway, something squeezing his heart as he stared at his daughter who was fast asleep, her sweet little body cuddled against Keely.

And Keely was asleep, too, each of them holding the other tightly.

'Phoebe's a very lucky girl, Mr Jordan,' the ward nurse said softly, her eyes resting on the pair in the bed. 'To have someone who loves her as much as that. Dr Thompson's in a great deal of pain but she insisted on reading to your daughter and cuddling her in the bed. When she heard that you were still busy downstairs she was determined that the child would sleep with her until you were available.'

For the first time in his adult life Zach felt a lump building in his throat, and gave a cough to clear it.

'You're right, of course,' he said gruffly. 'Phoebe is lucky.'

Totally exhausted from the events of the day, he gave a nod of thanks to the ward nurse and stepped quietly into the darkened room.

He wanted to make sure that he was there when they both woke up.

Still half-asleep Keely suddenly realised that she was hot and then bit back a gasp of pain as a little body wriggled onto her burnt arm.

'OK, young lady…' Zach's deep voice came from right beside her and almost immediately Phoebe was lifted out of the bed. 'Sorry about that. I was waiting for her to wake up but I must have drifted off. Are you all right?'

Keely winced and managed a smile. 'I'm great,' she lied, trying to ignore the pain in her throat, her chest and her hand.

'Keekee hurt,' Phoebe said solemnly, her thumb in her mouth. 'Keekee poorly. Daddy cuggle Keekee.'

Keely met Zach's piercing gaze and immediately looked away, a hot flush spreading over her cheeks. Help. She didn't need the matchmaking attempts of a toddler, that was for sure!

'Daddy cuggle,' Phoebe said firmly, and Zach gave a grin and sat down on the edge of the bed, his daughter on his lap.

'Everyone seems to be matchmaking, don't they? First Ally and now Phoebe. Maybe it's time we listened to them.' He put his fingers under her chin and forced her to look at him. 'There's something I want to say to you and I need to do it quickly before A and E or some other wretched department rings and tries to drag me away.'

Her heart started to thump. 'Wh-what?'

'I want to tell you about Catherine. It's time you knew the truth.' Zach's expression was grim and he lifted his daughter off the bed in an easy movement.

'You, young lady, are going to play with the nurses for five minutes while I talk to Keely.'

Keely watched him leave the room, her brain totally jumbled. *What was he going to say?* She wasn't sure she could stand hearing him tell her just how much he'd loved his wife. She just wasn't up to it.

He returned a few minutes later without Phoebe and closed the door firmly behind him.

Instead of sitting on the bed, he walked over to the window, his body tense as he looked out over the mountains.

'I don't really know where to start, except to say that what I'm going to tell you now is between you and me.' His voice was low and she had to strain to hear him. 'I've never said this to anyone else and I don't ever want Phoebe to find out the truth.'

Keely stared at him. *Find out what?* What didn't he want Phoebe to find out about? What was the man talking about?

'After I finished my surgical job with your father I took another surgical job in a different London hospital, and that's where I met Catherine.' There was a slight pause. 'She was an orthopaedic surgeon and a very good one. In fact, she was brilliant. I admired her work, we went out a few times and then one night we'd both had a bit too much to drink and—well, let's just say that the result was Phoebe. She was a complete accident.'

Keely lay still, wanting to ask questions but not knowing where to start.

'But…I thought you were in love with her?'

'Well, I wasn't.' Zach turned round to face her,

his broad shoulders blocking out most of the light in the little room. 'We were just colleagues really. But I respected her and we had plenty in common—or so I thought. I really believed we could make it work.'

'She was pleased to be pregnant?'

'Pleased? Catherine?' Zach gave a laugh that rang with bitterness. 'Catherine was a career-woman, through and through. She'd made up her mind never to have children. She was even considering being sterilised but, of course, I didn't know that when I met her. So, no, she was not pleased when she found out she was pregnant. She wanted a termination.'

Keely gasped, her eyes wide with horror. 'Oh, Zach…'

'I talked her out of it.' Zach's voice was gruff. 'I promised that I'd help, that she could still work, that we could have a nanny for some of the time. I asked her to marry me.'

Keely swallowed. 'And she did…'

'Yes, she did.' Zach sighed and rubbed his fingers over his rough jaw. 'But it was a mistake. I thought that once the baby arrived she'd settle down, but she was back at work two days after Phoebe was born.'

Keely gaped at him, unable to believe what she was hearing. *'Two days?'*

'Shocking, isn't it? She hired a nursery nurse and went back to work—full time.' Zach's expression was grim and his blue eyes were suddenly hard. 'And when I say full time, I mean full time. She was never at home.'

Keely was finding it hard to grasp. 'But Phoebe…'

Zach gave a derisive laugh. 'She wasn't interested in Phoebe. She didn't want to be with Phoebe. As far as Catherine was concerned, Phoebe was just something that could ruin her career. Catherine wasn't there when she took her first step or when she said her first word—and she didn't care.'

'Zach, I'm so sorry.' Keely's voice was soft. She found it impossible to imagine anyone not being interested in their child. 'So what happened?'

He shrugged. 'Catherine spent less and less time at home so I spent more time at home to compensate. In the end I gave up on a career in surgery and switched to A and E because the hours were better. It meant that on most days I could be home to bath Phoebe and we had most weekends together.'

'And what happened to Catherine?'

Zach's jaw tightened. 'We muddled along for a while and then she accepted a job in the States—'

'The States? You mean *America*?' Keely's voice was a horrified squeak and he gave a wry smile.

'Why not? She was offered a plum position in Boston and she decided to move.'

Keely shook her head, unable to believe what she was hearing. 'And leave her family?'

He shrugged. 'As far as Catherine was concerned, she didn't have a family. We were just a hindrance. By then our marriage had totally disintegrated and we barely saw each other. Even when she wasn't working she spent most of her time at the hospital.'

'So she moved to America?'

'No.' He shook his head. 'A week before she was due to go she was called out to a major accident on the motorway. She crashed in the fog. And that was it.'

Keely closed her eyes. 'Oh, Zach…'

'And do you know the hardest thing of all?' Zach's voice was conversational, as if he were talking about the weather, not the death of his wife. 'The fact that everyone felt sorry for me. They all assumed I must be devastated. And I wasn't. It was a tragedy of course—for her. But for us?' He paused and shook his head slowly. 'It sounds callous, I know, but in a way her death made it easier for me and for Phoebe. But, of course, no one knew that.'

'No. They couldn't possibly have understood.' She lifted her eyes to his, knowing that everything she felt for him was there for him to see. 'But I understand. Telling Phoebe that her mother died when she was little is going to be so much easier than telling her that her mother never wanted her and had moved to the other side of the world.'

His eyes locked with hers. 'Precisely.'

She took a deep breath. It was almost too much to take in.

He hadn't loved Catherine.

'We did all assume that you were devastated because you lost your wife,' she said, struggling to sit more upright in the bed. 'We all assumed you loved her so much you could never love another woman again.'

'I know what people assumed.' He gave a shrug. 'And I let them carry on with their false assumptions. It protected Phoebe from the truth. That our marriage was a sham and her mother didn't want her.'

Keely was still confused. 'But you told me that you had nothing left to give any woman after Catherine,' she asked quietly. 'I don't understand. If you weren't grieving for your wife, what was stopping you having a relationship with someone else?'

'A lack of trust. After everything that happened with Catherine I wasn't in a hurry to trust another woman again. Phoebe's happiness was at stake.' Zach paced across the room, his hands thrust deep into his pockets. 'And I suppose the truth was that I never met anyone I was remotely interested in.' He stopped dead and lifted his head to look at her. 'Until you came back into my life.'

Suddenly the room went very still and Keely forgot to breathe.

What was he saying?

'I tried to keep you at a distance but the chemistry between us is so strong it was impossible…' His voice was hoarse and his eyes burned into hers. 'Let's be honest for a moment. There was always something between us, Keely. Always. Even when you were young, we connected. When I came to stay in your house it was *you* that I enjoyed spending time with.'

She gave an awkward laugh. 'I was an irritating teenager—'

'No.' He shook his head and walked towards her. 'You were never that. You were smiley and enthusiastic and ridiculously caring about everything and everyone around you. When you proposed to me that night I suddenly realised that you were growing up fast. Frighteningly fast.'

'I should never have said what I said.' She blushed. 'I can't even begin to imagine what you must have thought of me.'

His eyes were warm. 'I thought you were gorgeous and I was flattered.'

'But you never visited us again...'

There was a long silence. 'Because I didn't trust myself,' he said finally. 'You were at a very dangerous age. You weren't a child any more and I knew that you needed space to spread your wings. So I kept my distance. I never thought you'd come back into my life.'

'But I did.'

'You did, indeed. And you kept trying to prove to me how grown up you were.'

'I had to. You thought I was a child,' Keely reminded him and he shook his head with a smile.

'Oh, no, I didn't. From the moment I saw you sitting in the lecture theatre, hiding your face behind your hand, I knew that you were all woman. And, believe me, keeping my hands off you nearly drove me crazy.'

He'd wanted her all along?

'So why did you keep saying that you couldn't get involved with me?'

There was a long silence and a muscle worked in his lean jaw. 'I didn't want to get involved with another career-woman.'

She stared at him, taking in what he'd just said.

And suddenly everything fell into place.

Dear Lord, he'd thought she was like Catherine.

No wonder he'd wanted to keep her at a distance.

Now was the time to confess.

'Zach, about my career—this cardiology job...' She hesitated and he sat down on the bed.

'Don't worry about it. I think it's great that you want to be a cardiologist.' His voice was gruff. 'Career or no career, you're nothing like Catherine and I should have realised that straight away. But I suppose I was carrying too much hurt and bitterness to be able to see things objectively.'

Keely licked her lips. 'Zach, I should have talked to you about my career earlier—'

'Your career isn't what matters,' he said quietly, taking her hand in his and stroking her blonde hair away from her face. 'What really matters is the way I feel about you. And the way I think you feel about me. I love you, Keely. I love you with all my heart. I want you to marry me. I want you to be my wife and Phoebe's mother.'

She couldn't believe what she was hearing. Couldn't believe that he meant it.

Tears filled her eyes and spilled out onto her cheeks. 'Oh, Zach...'

'Don't cry!' He gave a low curse and brushed the tears away with his thumb. 'Dammit, sweetheart, I can't bear to see you cry.'

'I'm crying because I'm happy.' She sniffed, rubbing her cheeks with the palm of her hand. 'I can't believe you're really saying this. You'd better pinch me so that I can be sure I'm not dreaming.'

'I think your poor body has suffered enough trauma in the last twenty-four hours without me pinching you,' Zach said dryly, the corners of his mouth lifting slightly. 'I'm in suspense here, Keely. Can I take it that the answer is yes?'

She nodded, the tears starting again. 'Of course it's yes. I've loved you since I was sixteen. You know that. I just can't believe that you really love me, too. That night we—you know...' She broke off, embarrassed, and he gave her a sexy grin that made her insides melt.

'I do know.'

'I couldn't believe it when you didn't mention it the next morning. Then you asked me to move out—'

'I know.' His smile faded and his voice was suddenly serious. 'I must have hurt you very badly. But you have to try and understand what I was thinking. After that incredible night I came downstairs and the first person I spoke to was your father, telling me that you'd got an interview and how clever you were. All of a sudden it was Catherine all over again.'

Keely stared at him, horrified. 'You *do* think I'm like Catherine?'

He gave a lopsided smile. 'No. I know you're nothing like Catherine. You're gentle, warm and kind with wonderful values and a fantastic way with children. But you're also very clever. Cleverer than you realise. You could go far, Keely. You could do whatever you wanted to do.'

Her eyes filled again. 'What I really want is for you to tell me you love me again. You didn't convince me the first time.'

'Then I'd better try harder.' He reached for a tissue. 'Keely Thompson, I love you. Madly. With all my heart and soul. But, please, stop crying or they'll throw me out for upsetting a patient.'

She wanted him to carry on telling her that he loved her…

'But, Zach…' A thought had suddenly struck her and she gasped. 'What about your home? Where will we live?'

Had his house burned to the ground? She hadn't even asked about his lovely house.

He shrugged. 'I love the Lakes, I can't pretend I don't. But I accept that you'll be happier in London, so that's where we'll go. But I'd like to keep the house here, too. For weekends and holidays.'

Her eyes widened and a smile touched her full mouth. 'The house is OK? It didn't burn down?'

He shook his head. 'It'll be fine once the builders have spent some time there.'

'That's great. Because I don't just want to use it for weekends and holidays.' She looked him in the eye. 'I love it here, too. I want to stay here. I want to live in your house.'

He stared at her and his hand tightened on hers. 'I can't ask you to do that—'

'You don't have to,' she said simply. 'I don't want to move to London. And I don't want to be a cardiologist. I had doubts right from the beginning. That was why I came up here. I needed to escape from the pressure of my family. They mean well but they're so forceful that I'd lost sight of what I really wanted to do. I was so swept along with what everyone else wanted that I'd lost track of what makes me happy.'

'But why the hell didn't you say something?' He stared at her, astounded. 'To be honest, I thought it was an odd choice of career for you. Why didn't you tell me how you felt?'

'Lots of reasons.' She gave him a sheepish smile. 'Because I thought you liked career-women. Because I wanted to prove to you that I was an adult and that seemed like a pretty good way, and because—' She broke off and his eyes narrowed.

'Because what?'

She blushed at his gentle prompt. 'Because I knew that I was in love with you right from the start, and I thought that if I kept telling you that I was going to London I'd throw you off the scent.'

'You certainly did that!' He groaned and shook his head. 'What a pair of idiots! I guessed you were in love with me—you're not that great at hiding your feelings, my love—but I assumed that your career was so important you wanted to go to London anyway.'

She shook her head. 'I really, really don't want to go to London. I know exactly what I want to do, and it's not cardiology.'

'Go on.' His voice was hoarse and she smiled, knowing how pleased he'd be by what she had to tell him.

'I want to be a GP, Zach. I decided that night we had dinner with Ally. I loved hearing about what she did and I knew that I wanted to do it, too. You know I'm no good at just dealing with patients for a short time. I'm too interested in them. I want to be involved in their lives and know everything there is to know about them.'

Zach stroked a hand across his face and let out a long breath. 'You're really sure you want to be a GP? You don't want to go to London?'

'No.' She shook her head. 'I don't want to go anywhere. I just want to stay here with you and Phoebe.'

There was a long silence while he digested what she'd just said and his eyes searched hers.

'I don't want you to accuse me of ruining a brilliant career.'

'What's brilliant about it if it's something I don't want to do? I don't want that sort of career,' she assured him. 'I've got everything I want right here.'

A slow smile spread across his handsome face. 'In that case, I'll make some calls and get you on the GP rotation here as soon as possible.'

'Ah.' He hadn't heard *all* her news yet. 'I'm not sure about that, Zach.'

He frowned. 'But you said—'

'I know what I said.' She looked at him calmly, enjoying teasing him just a little. 'But there are things I have to do first.'

'Like what?'

'Like be a mother to Phoebe,' she said quietly, taking his hand and looking deep into his eyes. 'No more nannies, Zach. Not for a while anyway. I want to be there for her—get to know her.'

'But that would mean giving up work.' He looked at her, clearly stunned and touched by her proposition. 'Are you saying you want to give up work to look after my daughter?'

'*Our* daughter, Zach. She's our daughter now,' Keely reminded him, searching for the right way to say what she had to say. 'And I want to have some time on my own with her before—well, I'll be giving up work pretty soon anyway, so I thought I may as well do it now, when my time in A and E comes to an end.'

There was a long silence.

'Giving up work?' His voice cracked slightly. 'Why will you be giving up work?'

Keely glanced towards the door to make sure that no one could hear them and then gave him a shy smile. 'Because, Mr Jordan, thanks to the over-whelming chemistry between us, we were a little careless one night...'

Zach stared at her, stunned into silence. 'Are you trying to tell me that you're *pregnant*?'

She nodded and then her happy smile faltered slightly. 'Is it—? You don't mind—do you?'

'Mind?'

He looked totally shocked.

'Zach, for goodness' sake!' She stared at him anxiously. 'I know we didn't plan this, but...'

Finally he seemed to stir himself, his eyes clouded with worry.

'Are you all right? I mean, the fire—'

'Everything's fine, Zach,' she reassured him quickly. 'I talked to the doctor and he's examined me.'

'Thank God.' Zach let out a long breath and shook his head. 'A baby...'

'You're not angry?'

'Angry? It's the best thing that could have happened,' he said softly, leaning forward and kissing her gently on the mouth. 'I can't believe this. I was so carried away that night I wasn't even thinking straight.'

'Nor me. But I'm thinking straight now, and I don't want to start my GP rotation yet. I want to be at home for now, Zach, if that's all right with you. There's plenty of time to go back to work when they're older. What do you think?'

'What do I think?' He brushed her hair away from Keely's face with gentle fingers, everything he felt for her showing in his eyes. 'I think you are the most wonderful woman in the world. And I'm the luckiest man on the planet. All of a sudden I seem to have acquired another child and a wife. My perfect family.'

'And a mother for Phoebe,' Keely reminded him with a smile.

'Yes.' His mouth tilted into an answering smile and he nodded slowly. 'And a mother for Phoebe.'

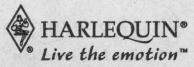

A **brand-new** *Maitland Maternity* story!

MAITLAND MATERNITY

Adopt
–a–Dad

by

Marion Lennox

The second in a quartet of *Maitland Maternity* novels connected by a mother's legacy of love.

When Michael Lord's secretary, Jenny Morrow, found herself widowed and pregnant, the confirmed bachelor was determined to help. Michael had an idea to make things easier for Jenny and her baby immediately— a temporary husband!

Coming to a retail outlet near you in October 2003.

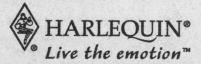

**Treat yourself to some festive
reading this holiday season
with a fun and jolly volume...**

T E M P O R A R Y
Santa

**Two full-length novels
at one remarkable low price!**

Favorite authors

Cathy Gillen
THACKER

Leigh
MICHAELS

**Two sexy heroes find true love at Christmas
in this romantic collection.**

Coming in November 2003—just in time for the holidays!

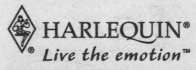

HARLEQUIN®
Live the emotion™

Visit us at www.eHarlequin.com

BR2TS

**From Silhouette Books comes
an exciting NEW spin-off to *The Coltons!***

PROTECTING PEGGY

by award-winning author
Maggie Price

When FBI forensic scientist Rory Sinclair checks into Peggy Honeywell's inn late one night, the sexy bachelor finds himself smitten with the single mother. While Rory works undercover to solve the mystery at a nearby children's ranch, his feelings for Peggy grow…but will his deception shake the fragile foundation of their newfound love?

Coming in December 2003.

THE COLTONS
FAMILY. PRIVILEGE. POWER.

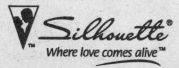

Where love comes alive™